COPPER LIES

COPPER
LIES

ALLI PRINCE

The Pearl

PEARLBOOKS.CO

DEVELOPMENTAL EDITOR
Brad Pauquette

COPY EDITOR
Vella Karman

BOOK DESIGNER
R.J. Catlin

COVER ART
Levi Matthews

Copyright © 2024 by Alli Prince

Paperback: 978-1-960230-11-9
Ebook: 978-1-960230-12-6

To my mentor, Brad Pauquette.
Without you, this book wouldn't exist and I'd probably be
working at a Dairy Queen right now.
Thank you for teaching me the craft of writing, but more
so, for teaching me what grace looks like.

I SAT WITH MY BACK against the wooden church pew and did everything I could to avoid the Mother Mary's cold, hard eyes. It was a perfect depiction of her, or so I assumed. She was made of finely carved marble. I watched the light glint off her round cheeks and the bow of her cupid lips. She seemed to carry the baby in her arms as though it was light as a feather. She cradled it against the base of her neck. Her chin was tilted up, and her pupils were aimed down toward the congregation.

"As the Scriptures say, the harlots, fornicators, and—and adulterers shall not inherit the kingdom of God," the preacher spoke from the front. Periodically, he'd thump his right hand against the Bible in his left as if the words that droned out of his mouth and cluttered in the rafters above us were actually making a point. "And—and I say it again, if those such people aren't welcome in the kingdom, then they shan't be welcome in such a place as our good and perfect town of Kesterfield, now should they?"

I held in a yawn and shifted as the congregation applauded. My back had a pinch in it.

It's all your fault.

I clenched my teeth and ignored the insidious whisper that came from deep inside my head. I looked down at my skirts and picked at a stray string.

It's all your fault.

Logically, the idea that there was *any* blame in my situation was nonsense.

"Amen."

I jumped as the congregation stood, and quickly, I stood with them. I slipped from the pew and smoothed down my green and purple patched skirts. I'd just about made it to the back of the church, past the people quickly gathering and chattering, when a hand fell on my shoulder.

"Lillian, dear, where is your uncle this fine morning?"

I put a smile in place and slowly turned around. Ah, yes, the good mayor of Kesterfield—Albert Bamford.

He was a large man with a stomach that pushed against his striped button-up vest. He kept his mustache oiled and hid his balding scalp underneath the brim of his bowler hat. He'd been mayor far longer than I had lived in the perfect little town of Kesterfield. I continued to smile, my hands folded in front of me.

"Good morning, Mayor Bamford," I bowed my head. My two braids swooshed past my shoulders as I did. Subtly, I shifted them behind my ears once more. "The good Professor Booker is off on another adventure. For his birthday. You see, our benefactor, Miss Witherstine, has gifted him a trip across the countryside to make new acquaintances and find inspiration for his inventions."

"Oh," he nodded and smoothed his mustache between two

meaty fingers. "And he's left you here? Alone? Hardly a re-spectable thing for a young flower like yourself to be left alone, what with the beasts about..."

I pressed harder into my grin, my fists curling around my skirts.

"Well, somebody *capable* had to look after his inventions and experiments, didn't they?" I asked.

He's left you for good. It's all your fault.

I forced a breath in through my nose and let it out through parted lips. I'd resisted the urge to beg to go with him on his trip—and now regretted not asking at least once. Would the sting of that rejection have hurt less than the dull pain of this conversation? I would never know. I swallowed and nodded toward the mayor—who had turned to the lovely Miss Cordington and was already deep in conversation. Just past them, the Mother Mary stared down at me, her eyes half-lidded and lips pursed as though she were smothering a cruel smile.

Promptly, I turned, my braids swishing behind me, and headed toward the two large oak doors at the back of the church. I wove past groupings of people chattering and then finally slipped outside into the fresh Sunday morning air.

My skirts fluttered in the wind. I looked over the perfect town of Kesterfield. Professor Booker's mark could be seen on nearly every single home—in the brass pipes that lined almost every corner of every house. They twisted along eaves and then down into the ground, periodically letting small bursts of steam into the air. His hand could be seen in the church bell, which was nestled in the steeple on the top of the church above me. It had been turned into a speaker and sat on its side. Every invention—every new improvement in society—they were created from his genius.

3

"It is now twelve o'clock. Please enjoy your Sunday afternoon," the voice crackled through the metallic speaker and echoed through the town.

I walked down the steps of the church and came to a halt as the trolley bustled down the lane. Instead of wheels, this trolley had been outfitted with large mechanical legs positioned at each corner of the cart. Gears on each leg shifted and clicked as the trolley strolled forward. Steam escaped in puffs from the pipes in the back of the cart, and a whistle blew from the front as it passed the church. I watched as it rounded the curved corner of Basker Avenue and vanished from sight. I barreled forward across Main Street and to the market.

It's all your fault.

I huffed. It was *not*, but there was only so long I could argue with the whispers in my head.

I strolled past the market stalls and stopped at a stand that held freshly baked goods. I inhaled the fresh scent of baked bread and eyed a blueberry muffin.

"Baked just this morning!" Mr. Bennett leaned against the counter. He was a kindly, plump man with warm red cheeks and a thick head of blond hair.

"I can tell," I stepped forward. My eyes flicked down to his right arm—a mangle of brass and metal where his hand should have been. A year ago, there'd been an accident with a beast from the quarry. I pressed my lips together and focused back on the baked goods.

"Please—take a muffin, free o' charge," he smiled.

"Oh—no, you worked hard on—" I snapped my mouth shut as he pressed the small blueberry muffin toward me. I looked at his outstretched hand, the sunlight glinting off the

4

brass fingers. I looked back up at him. "Please, Mr. Bennett, I couldn't—"

"Least I could do after all the Professor's done for me." He smiled, his eyes shining with warmth. My stomach churned.

So lazy—taking credit for the Professor's hard work. You're horrible.

"And I am not the Professor, just his niece." I dipped my head. "Good day."

Quickly, I turned and stalked away. I passed the many stands in the marketplace and couldn't help but see Professor Booker's influence on each one. A large machine that counted coins sat on each counter and bore his signature brass coloring. The mechanical canes that elderly men used to walk or to swat at the legs of noisy children were of his design. The ache in my chest grew with each invention I saw.

A shout came from the forest edge. A group of men varying in age and size stood around a large creature on the ground. They wore cool green cloaks, a badge of honor as the town's Defense Team. I rolled my eyes.

"The beast is slain!" Albert Jr., the mayor's son, called out, his hands cupped around his bearded chin. "All is well!"

At their feet was a beast. My eyes widened, and slowly, I approached, studying the creature. Its reptilian face was smashed into the ground, its two eyes gouged out. Ruby-red blood trickled from the gaping holes. The scales—hard as iron—shimmered in the sunlight, its long snakelike body curled. The creatures didn't often come up from the quarry, which was miles outside the town line. But sometimes the smell of food from the morning market enticed them just enough. Thus, our valiant protectors, The Defense Team, were ready at any hour of the day to protect us.

I pursed my lips and stared at the creature. It was a good thing they were better at defending the town than they were at naming themselves.

"Good afternoon, Lillian Booker!"

My eyes shot up from the creature to Albert Jr.'s charming smile.

"Where is the good Professor—"

I turned away and quickly walked past him and out of the market. There was no need to repeat useless conversations.

Besides, I had important projects to work on. After all, it wasn't often Professor Booker went away for a week, especially not a week before his birthday—a townwide celebration, of course—practically a national holiday for us.

I grinned, tucked my braids behind my ears, and rushed down the cobblestone path toward the back roads of Kesterfield. I was going to make sure that this was the Professor's best birthday of all! My boots hit the dirt and I continued to run.

I was his apprentice for a reason.

It took a little less than ten minutes for me to arrive at our home. The scenery quickly changed from posh and perfect businesses and homes to the hills that swelled like ocean waves. Professor Booker's manor sat nestled between sweeping farmlands and fields. The manor was tall, with cracked purple and green paint along the trim. He'd inherited it from his older brother, who'd inherited it from his father, who'd inherited it from *his* father, and so on and so forth.

A stone wall encased the property, split only by a wrought iron gate. I stepped through the gate and onto the gravel pathway. In front of the house, a crisscross of overgrown gardens and wild vegetation threatened to overtake the path. I walked to the left, around the side of our home, and toward the back. In front of me was a large barren field, and at the very end, next to the forest edge, stood a large windmill. I stood for a moment and watched the cloth wings slowly spin in the summer breeze. This was Professor Booker's workshop.

I rolled up my sleeves as I stalked across the field and then stepped through the wooden door into Professor Booker's workshop.

Above me, the wooden beams connecting to the wings outside creaked as they turned. Copper and brass pipes cluttered the space below them in a zigzagged maze. Eventually all of the pipes led back to the large furnace in the middle of the circular room.

Though the inside of the windmill was a large circular space, it felt cramped due to the many piles of Professor Booker's various projects. They lined every shelf, sat upon every workbench, and took up large sections of the floor.

Each project sat in the open, shining in the dim light. Immediately to my left and jutting out from the stone walls, a staircase curved upwards. That was where the Professor sent any project he couldn't bear to look at anymore. At least, that was before I moved in. Now, it held those projects *and* any project I was working on. I had very few compared to the Professor, and even fewer that were considered decent by any measure… But still, a little corner in the attic space above was mine and mine alone.

I snatched my apron off the peg on the wall, then walked past the large stacks of metal sheets and the buckets of screws toward the back. Atop Professor Booker's workbench was a purple cloth thrown over a lumpy figure. A small metallic claw poked from underneath the edge of the cloth.

"I'm back!" I grinned and set the apron on the table next to the figure.

I rubbed the cloth between my thumb and forefinger. Then, gently, I lifted it up and set it to the side. The sunbeams from the circular window above us trickled in and shone over the brass and copper statue.

Its head was made of discarded pennies, gears, and wires that I'd welded together to form a reptilian shape. The eyes were made of two marbles I'd swiped from the living room, one a deep shade of amber and the other a lightning yellow. They were set inside metal spoons, bent and welded in place.

Bits of scrap metal had become tiny individual scales that traveled down the lizardlike creature and formed a large tail that curled around its clawed feet. Its snout had two wires trailing down in a curl. A brass door hinge connected its jaws. Inside the mouth and embedded in the jaw, I'd screwed in bits of shimmering broken glass, discarded nails, and pieces of copper.

Once in action, the creature would be able to relight the furnace in mere seconds—and look amazing while it did it!

I stuck my fingers in the jaw, careful to avoid the sharp edges. With a grunt, I pried it open. The hinges squeaked loudly as I did. I looked into the mouth. Deep in the back of its throat was a small tube with a lighter hovering over the opening.

I'd wrestled this project down from the workshop's attic the second after Professor Booker had bid me goodbye. I removed my arm from the dragon's maw and thought back to this morning.

We had stood in the entryway of Professor Booker's manor. His usual frizzy white hair had been combed back into submission and placed under a top hat. His jacket was newly bought.

"Now, Miss Witherstine shall be watching over you while I am away," his voice was thick and gruff as he adjusted the settings on his mechanical cane. The gears shifted and clicked as he pulled the brass lever. I watched as the metal staff shuddered and adjusted in height. Professor Booker grinned past his white mustache, leaned against the cane, and looked at me.

"Come now, Lillian." He smiled. "I'll only be off for a week. Then we can continue to experiment on the stones. I give you my word. You and me…we're a team."

He had mistaken my excitement for his birthday gift as anxiety at his departure. How funny.

"Please enjoy yourself." I gently curtsied, my head tipped to the ground. I heard his footsteps travel over the soft carpet, and in a moment, I was wrapped up in his arms. My eyes fluttered shut. I took in the scent of oil mixed with a deep peppermint. My forehead came to the top of his shoulder, and I resisted the urge to rest against him. Gently, I cleared my throat and patted his arm, then stepped away.

"Ha! Will you miss me?" Professor Booker leaned forward, his eyes sparkling. I felt a smile prod its way onto my face as I crossed my arms and stuck my nose in the air.

"Now, Professor, what on earth is there to miss?" I'd asked. *Evidently, a lot. You're pathetic.*

I frowned and rubbed the metallic claw of the beast. I didn't miss him—no, I was just antsy about finishing up my projects.

The workshop door swung open behind me. I snatched the cloth and threw it over the beast.

"Mornin', Lilly!" James, Professor Booker's original assistant, called as he stepped into the workshop. I felt heat rise to my cheeks and I sucked in a breath, then turned around to face him. James stood just inside the workshop. He grabbed his apron from the peg on the wall and threw it over his head. He smiled, his grin lopsided and his cheeks dusted with freckles. Though we were the same age, he stood a head taller than me. He smoothed his mid-length blond hair out of his eyes and I quickly turned away.

You'll never be a better assistant to the Professor than James.

"It's *Lillian*, James. Men shouldn't address a lady so casually," I reprimanded as I set about pretending to be busy. I grabbed my apron and threw it over my head.

"And since when have you been a lady?" he snorted. Then, a second later, he said, "Hey, these are new!"

I glanced up, my hands tangled in the apron strings as I tried to tie them together behind me. James had wandered over to a large bookcase stacked between a wooden bench and sheets of metal. I clicked my tongue and let the strings fall to my side as I walked over to him.

Four glowing rocks sat on the middle shelf behind a glass pane built into the wooden case. I slowly placed a hand on the pane, which was cold to the touch.

"They are...recent discoveries," I finally answered. I let my hand fall and took a step back.

James peered closer, eyes wide. "Where'd you find them?"

My hands itched to touch the rocks—to figure out exactly what they were and why they glowed the way they did.

"The quarry," I answered. James snapped his attention to me and I rolled my eyes. "We were perfectly safe... The Professor brought his arm-cannon."

James gave a low hum and turned back to the rocks. "Why're they glowing?"

I shrugged. "I don't know."

Of the four rocks we'd found, each glowed a peculiar and different color.

The stone on the far left glowed a turquoise blue. Its shape seemed to be a crudely cut triangle, and if you looked closely, you could see it floated a couple of inches off the shelf.

The second stone glowed a deep and rich purple. It seemed to be a circle or perhaps an octagon. A small, thin vine grew from the top of the circle.

The third stone glowed a deep maroon red and resembled a closed fist more than any particular shape.

The fourth and final stone glowed an icy white. Tiny white flakes had begun to spread on the bottom right corner of the glass pane set in the bookcase. The stone was small and round, like a ball.

"Put your hand on the glass," I whispered. He raised a single questioning eyebrow but obeyed. He sucked in a sharp breath and looked at me. I grinned. "Weird, right?"

He nodded and took a step back. I looked at the stones and bit my lip.

"Perhaps bio-luminescent properties are within the stones themselves…" I muttered, tapping my chin.

I froze as the straps to my apron tugged. James stood behind me and tied them into a neat bow. I pressed my lips tight together, my heart fluttering in my chest as his fingers brushed against my back. Once he'd finished, I tucked a braid behind my ear and stepped away toward the workbenches.

"So, how was morning service? Oh—before I forget," James smacked his forehead, then pulled out a worn yellow letter from his pocket. "Professor Booker stopped in the shop on his way out—said to give this to you."

"A letter?" I asked. I stepped forward. "Why did he give it to you?"

"Because of the two of us, *I'm* the most responsible. You'd probably shove it into your pockets and forget its existence until laundry day." James playfully bumped my shoulder. I bit my lip to keep the smile off my face and placed my hands on my hips.

"Well, give it here," I held out my hand. He passed me the letter and then leaned against the edge of the workbench with a grin.

"Go on, open it. I've been curious all morning."

"And what makes you think you have any right to a lady's private postage," I stuck my nose in the air and pressed the letter to my chest. "Shoo!"

James shook his head and grabbed a broom. He eyed me as he began to sweep. I walked over to the bench with my dragon and hoisted myself up to sit next to it. I looked down at the yellow paper. My name was scrawled on the front in swirling black cursive. I traced my finger along the letter 'L', then opened the letter.

Dear Lillian,

This is the first time we've been apart since you've come to live at Booker Lane. I trust you will complete these two tasks I've left you.

The first. Please help out our benefactor, Miss Witherstine, with whatever you can. I've left you in her charge, so you will be expected to attend her bimonthly tea at one o'clock today.

Be presentable.

The second. Do not experiment on the magical rocks we found in the quarry. They are dangerous. Do not even look at them.

You should not worry about the chores and upkeep of the inventions. I've left that to James.

Yours,
Professor Booker

"Oh, James!" I pressed my lips together and looked toward the clock on top of the wooden cabinet. It was a quarter to one. Then I glanced down at my clothes. Dirt marred the hems of my skirts, and the sleeves of my blouse sported small black oil smears.

"What's wrong?" James asked as I shoved the letter into my pocket.

"I'm going to be late—why didn't you give this to me sooner!" I hissed and wrestled with the strings on my apron.

"Late?" James set down the broom and walked toward me. He grabbed a string and tugged, the bow coming undone, and I threw the apron and letter onto the ground.

"Stay away from my things—and don't touch the stones!" I called as I ran toward the door. I'd attend this tea party, but then nothing would keep me from completing Professor Booker's birthday present.

I STOOD WITH MY HANDS clasped around the metal pole, gripping it to stay aboard the trolley as it rumbled up the street. Puffs of steam blew from exposed brass pipes. With each step the trolley took, the cart tilted from side to side. Professor Booker was currently experimenting with smoother modes of transportation. While the trolley did prove to be a bit of a bumpy ride, I found I liked the rough characteristics. It wasn't perfect, unlike the rest of Kesterfield. This trolley was like me in a way.

The trolley had taken me past sweeping farmlands, through the bustling town, and all the way to the other side of Kesterfield, to Creekstone Manor, in a little less than five minutes.

As we rumbled over the cobblestone lanes, one could already hear the needless chatter of fine society. We rounded the corner and came to the front of Creekstone Manor. It was hidden behind a large stone wall. From where I was, I could only see the top of a large oak tree nestled in the back gardens, and just behind it, the roof of the three-story estate.

Carriages carried women in fancy outfits to the gate,

and they chatted amiably with one another as they strolled through the stone archway and into the gardens. I looked down at my new dress—the one Professor Booker had laid out for me. It was simple compared to any of the other dresses at the party. A nice pale blue with a purple ribbon.

You're simplistic. Boring. Lame.

I shook my head and marched forward. I walked behind two plump women, their hair tied in fancy updos lined with flowers and pearls. Feathers poked out on opposite sides, mirroring each other, and their skirts swished as they strutted up the cobblestone walkway. I had no such trinkets to bind myself with and had kept my hair in two braids.

Though I'd seen the manor three times before, each time I found that the sight of it caught me off guard.

The wooden paneling along the sides of the manor was a pale pink. The trim, a delicate white, held each edge of the home perfectly and contrasted with the inky black of the steep gabled roof. On the front right corner of the manor was a large turret. Black spikes swirled intricately along the edge of the roof—mostly to discourage the birds from nesting, I assumed.

I swallowed and took a step into the house.

"Lillian, darling!" a shrill voice pierced my ears. I resisted the urge to wince and turned toward it in a calculated twist.

"Miss Witherstine," I smiled. Her blonde hair was pulled back into a perfect bun. Pearls lined her neck and wrists. Her dress seemed to be the latest fashion, or really, I assumed so since it was Miss Witherstine. It was a blush pink with white lace along the bodice. I swallowed and took a step forward.

"Oh, how good it is to see you!" She kissed the air on either side of my cheek and I pulled back, eyebrows creasing.

She patted my head with a white-gloved hand. "How many times do I have to tell you? Call me Victoria, darling, please! Why, I was just telling Johnathon last week, you know—well, I have been telling him for some time, I've said, ever since you came under his wing, I've said, 'Johnathon, she is a young lady, and young ladies must be rounded in the ways of society.'"

My nose scrunched. "Yes, you have said that."

"I'm so very glad you've finally come to one of our bi-monthly tea gatherings." She smiled and wrapped her arm tightly around my shoulder. Then, at a stroll, she pulled me deeper into the party.

"Now, make yourself at home," she encouraged me as we entered the parlor. "And remember—Johnathon has asked me to keep an eye on you, so don't stray too far now."

The parlor was drowned in lavish decor. Bundles of flowers had been ripped from their homes in the dirt and strung together with shiny bits of ribbon and hung around the room. The golden chandelier hung, shimmering, from the ceiling. Plush couches were set all around the room. Surrounding them were tables with an array of sweets set on top of them.

I turned, eyebrows scrunched. "Hmm, yes, about that. I actually don't think—"

I pressed my lips together as I watched Miss Witherstine sweep away like a leaf in a stream, quickly surrounded by women and men of status. I looked at the large clock that hung on the wall. Its gnarled black hands pointed toward the one... I frowned and looked back at the chattering hoard of ladies and gentlemen, a question burning at the front of my mind.

How long did I have to stay?

I didn't know which was worse. The way that my lace collar scratched my neck, or the bumbling chatter that echoed around the large parlor.

You're going to be stuck here forever.

I bit down on my tongue and pressed a smile onto my lips as I stared out at the sea of people in front of me. I looked up toward the ceiling—twelve to fifteen feet, easily—and couldn't help but imagine how agreeable the room would be as a workshop rather than a parlor.

I stood next to the parlor window. My back brushed the satin curtains and my skirt stuck firmly out at my sides. I glanced around at the many occupants.

You don't belong here. You never will.

I subtly shrugged and glanced out the window behind me. The gardens sprawled out in magnificent splendor.

"My goodness, what a face."

It took me a moment to recognize that comment as one spoken out loud. I looked away from the window to see Iris, Miss Witherstine's ward. She had her hands folded gently in front of her and wore a pleasant smile. Her straight black hair was pulled back with a purple ribbon that perfectly matched the shade of her expensive-looking purple dress.

"What?" I asked.

"*Smile*, Lillian Booker," she came up beside me. "In a place like this, you are in more danger than you could ever realize."

"Danger?"

"The forest isn't the only place beasts reside. Surely you

should know this, as a *woman*, brought up in a place of *status*…" she spoke each word as though it were the first time I'd heard English. "You must realize something as subtle as a frown can be taken by the gossipers of Kesterfield and spun into such fantastic tales… Hasn't Mr. Booker taught you that?"

"*Professor*," I corrected. "And yes, he and Victoria—"

"*Miss Witherstine*," Iris corrected with a biting smile. I faltered.

"Right… Miss Witherstine has made me quite aware of how a lady should behave." I paused. "But Professor Booker acts as he does and says as he pleases."

"*That* is because your uncle is a *man*." Iris stepped to the side. She glanced out toward the party through thick black lashes. "Men are entirely different creatures and, as such, live by a different set of rules."

I swallowed and glanced down at my shoes.

"Oh, don't frown, Lillian. It's not such a terrible thing. After all, we have different strengths." Lillian grinned. "Besides, the men have to protect us. We get splendid tea parties and make sure what they're protecting isn't squandered. It's not such a terrible world to live in, now is it? So chin up, and remember, even if you don't speak to anyone else at the party… Well, for your sake, I suggest you *smile*."

I watched as she turned, her inky black locks trailing behind her as she moved back into the crowd and disappeared. I set my teacup down on the side table and looked into my reflection in the window. I put on a smile.

You look like you're constipated.

My smile dropped. Behind me, I heard a hushed whisper as two women passed.

"Lillian Booker…I didn't know the Professor had ever married."

"Oh, he hasn't," the other whispered. "That's his niece—his brother, George Booker—passed on some time ago. It was only in the past year that the Professor was made aware of her existence and retrieved her from the orphanage she'd resided in."

"Oh, the poor thing!"

I still stared at the window, fidgeting with a loose string on my sleeve. I'd been in Kesterfield for a year and a half now, but I still remembered the long, dark trip into town like it was yesterday…

I had sat curled forward on the rough wooden bench of the cart next to the Professor. The cart had been unlike anything I'd ever seen. Lots of tiny gears, brass pipes, and a large furnace that took up the entire back of the cart. In front of Professor Booker was a large wooden board with different dials, switches, and buttons, as well as a metal steering wheel. Furious lightning streaked in the clouds far above us. I pulled the thin blanket around my shoulders and suppressed a shiver as I watched the forest's edge. A bush to my left rustled. I stared at it, eyes wide, until we'd passed it. A growl caught my ear, and I stiffened.

Next to me, the Professor cleared his throat. I looked up at him. His face was grim. There were creases in his forehead as his bushy white eyebrows drew together.

"You know, they can't get us," he said. "I invented this alarm system—a prototype, right now, but it will do the trick." He tapped a tiny whistle next to the steering wheel. "This alarm will go off the moment a beast is within range—and here, I've got weaponry to defend against such creatures. If any attack, I've got the means to protect us."

I frowned, doubt chewing at my stomach.

"You'll love Kesterfield," the Professor continued. He fiddled with the gears and levers on the machine. "They've got lovely roads and wonderful shops. Once we get in, we'll find you some proper dresses. You'll be invited to all sorts of parties, and our church is one of a kind! It really is the perfect little town."

I looked down at the brown frock I called a dress. "Won't they ask questions?" I whispered. People like me were not usually welcome in perfect little towns.

Another growl came from the forest and I sucked in a breath. The bushes moved, and next to us, the alarm let out a faint, high-pitched whistle.

"Say, why don't you just call me '*uncle*,' then? No one would be the wiser." The Professor grabbed his cane and held down the silver lever on the side. The end of the cane clicked open. I pulled my feet up into the seat with me and kept my eyes on the moving leaves.

"I don't think I'm comfortable with that," I whispered. The Professor leveled his cane with the cart, shut one eye, and pulled the lever. A bolt shot from the open end of the cane and vanished into the leaves. Something shrieked and then bounded away from us. I let go of my breath, and beside me, the Professor lowered his cane.

"Professor, then. Call me Professor," he had said.

I subtly glanced around the perfect room—with its perfect inhabitants and perfect smiles. I smoothed out my skirt and walked briskly across the parlor and toward the exit.

Nobody would care if you left. They didn't want you here in the first place.

I slipped past the door and into the hall. Quietly, I dodged around servants and maids, trailing my way toward the kitchens of Creekstone Manor. It was ever so nice of Miss Witherstine to invite me, whether or not I had a choice in accepting the invitation, but I had a birthday present to work on.

I slipped into the kitchen. Cooks bustled around carrying trays of pastries and cookies. It smelled heavenly. Chocolates and cakes were stacked high upon serving trays ready to go out into the party. These people—the chefs and cooks and maids and servants—they were the people I wanted to be with. The hard workers. The resilient of character.

I watched as they hesitated, unsure why I—a lady of social standing—had graced them with my presence.

"Miss, can I help you?" a maid approached.

"No—no thank you." I avoided their curious gazes and walked over the small white tiles of the kitchen floor and out the back door.

It shut behind me with a quiet click, and once again, I was alone. I didn't belong with the servants or with society.

The gardens of Creekstone Manor seemed to me almost as perfect as the manor itself. I scrunched my nose and walked down the stone steps. My boots crunched in the gravel pathway.

The flowers had each sprouted a perfect number of petals. The bushes had been mercilessly trimmed. I picked up the pace, stepped delicately over the babbling creek that trickled pleasurably through the gardens, and came to a patch of grass. A single lily stood apart from the rest of the flowers, and in front of me, a giant oak tree. I licked my lips and glanced back toward the manor.

Nobody will miss you.

I stuck my boot against the base of the tree and began to climb. I scrambled over the rough bark until I reached the first branch and hoisted myself up. Carefully, I balanced on the branch that spanned over the stone fence—the one that kept the imperfect chaos of nature and life at bay. I grinned, swung my legs up, and began to crawl forward. The tree shook as my weight shifted. Stray twigs and leaves scattered over the top of my hair.

I huffed, crept over the wall, and glanced down. The ground below was at a downward angle. A steep hill that went down and met a dirt path. The back roads of Kester-field. I swallowed. It was a far steeper drop than I had originally anticipated.

I shut my eyes. Slowly, I shifted so my lower half hung off the branch. I grit my teeth as I held myself up by my arms.

"*Breathe,*" I whispered and let go of the branch.

My stomach lurched into my throat and my heart squeezed. I shut my eyes and felt my braids fly toward the sky. I landed and rolled. My ankles stung as I struck the ground and tumbled down the grassy hill below. The world spun over and over until, finally, I came to rest at the bottom of the hill.

I took in a breath. The grass poked at my neck. The sky above me was clear except for the occasional fluffy cloud that sprawled lazily across the great blue sky. I smiled. I had escaped and nobody was the wiser.

I popped off the ground, dusted my dress, and set off down the road toward the workshop.

I walked briskly across the barren field and toward the workshop, my mind already racing with the tasks I had before me. Professor Booker's birthday present had yet to reach the standard of perfection I strove for, and yet, my mind was torn.

Professor Booker had said not to experiment on the stones. To not even look at them. But that didn't mean I couldn't *think* about them. How amazing would it be for the Professor to come back to a working dragon *and* theories to begin with?

We'd only found them a week before...

The rain had pelted us from above. I'd rested the large brass cannon on my hip and stared out at the darkness around us, one hand gripped the handle on the top of the cannon and the other gripped the back, one finger hovering over the slender metal trigger. Behind me, Professor Booker used a drill to dig deep into the slick rock sides of the quarry. We'd been at it for hours. I blinked the water from my eyes as I searched for any sign of a beast.

"Lillian—oh, look! Look!" His crazed exclamation had brought my attention from our surroundings to the small red stone in his hands. I'd lowered the cannon, eyes wide as I watched it pulse rhythmically in his hand. Thump-thump, thump-thump, thump-thump.

"What in the world?" I stepped toward him. The Professor grinned as he held up the stone.

"Here it is, Lillian," Professor Booker cheered. "Our answer to the beasts!"

I hadn't a clue what the Professor meant when he said that. It led one to wonder what his intentions were... If I knew what his intentions were, I could prepare what we'd need for the experiments we'd conduct. I slipped through the wooden door and froze. James stood just in front of the workbench, purple cloth in hand, staring at my dragon.

"Hey!" I yelped before I could stop myself. "What do you think you're doing?!"

James looked up with a grin. "This is so cool! Is this a dragon?"

I rushed forward, the door slamming shut behind me, and grabbed the other end of the purple cloth.

"Hey!" James held firm to the cloth, as I glowered up at him. "What's wrong?"

"Nothing," I smiled. "This is a private matter and was covered by a cloth for a reason, so if you don't mind—"

"I *do* mind—since when did Professor Booker make metal sculptures instead of inventions?" James held the cloth as I continued to tug, his eyes back on the dragon. I grit my teeth together. James stepped forward, gently tapping the marble eyes as he continued, "Unless, of course, this *is* an invention. But Professor Booker never tries to hide his…"

James let go of the cloth, and I quickly swiped it toward me. I held it to my chest and took a long, even breath. Slowly, James looked at me, eyes shining.

"*You* made this?" he asked. Warmth flooded my cheeks, and I stepped between him and the table. Quickly, I threw the purple cloth over the dragon.

"I told you—it's private!" I turned around to face him. James grinned.

"So it's a secret!" He stepped forward, peering around me, and I involuntarily backed into the workbench. My heart hammered in its cage, and I stared up at him with a scowl.

"It's none of your business!" I insisted. James shifted his weight, his thumbs resting just inside his pockets as he smirked.

"C'mon, out with it," he nodded toward the dragon. "What's it do?"

I clenched my fists and looked away. "It's...to heat up the furnace faster...for Professor Booker's birthday, so *yes*, it's a secret."

I stared at the ground and forced my trembling hands together.

"Lilly, this is fantastic!" James exclaimed.

I looked up at him and couldn't help the question that followed. "You really think so?"

"Of course!" James stepped around me and lifted the cloth. He leaned forward, his shoulder brushing mine. "Look at the detail—the design! The craftsmanship alone is impressive. How long have you been working on this?"

I fought the smile that was forcing its way onto my face. "Months, at this point. I've kept it hidden upstairs, but since Professor Booker is traveling, I figured I should take the opportunity to finish it up—to prove what I'm capable of."

"I mean—it's amazing. What more needs to be done on it?" James asked.

"Please, James," I rolled my eyes and crossed my arms. "It's not even close to done. I've a lot of all-nighters to pull to finish it by Professor Booker's—"

The door to the workshop slammed open. I jumped and flipped around. Miss Witherstine stood in the doorway, illuminated by the light now streaming in.

"Lillian," she hissed my name. Strands of hair had escaped her perfect bun. She stalked forward. "What on earth do you think you're doing in here?"

I stopped. "Miss Witherstine, I was—"

She halted as she caught sight of James. He leaned against the workbench, hiding the dragon with his body, his hands in his pocket.

"Miss Witherstine," he nodded his head once. She looked between the two of us and pressed her lips together into a firm line.

"James Cordington," Miss Witherstine inclined her head politely. "May I ask what the two of you are doing?"

James glanced over to me. His eyebrows raised a notch. "As Lillian was saying, we're just cleaning up."

Miss Witherstine's eyes flashed as she smiled. "Hmm, how wonderful. Well, perhaps Lillian and I can leave you to your work. I've something to discuss with her."

James shrugged with an ease I envied, grabbed the broom, and set back to sweeping.

"Lillian. Please come with me," she spoke primly, her words terse. I grimaced and, with a subtle roll of my eyes, followed her outside.

I EXPECTED A VERY SPECIFIC conversation to follow after being found with a boy the same age as me, alone in a secluded dusty old windmill.

And I already had a million reasons why Miss Witherstine's concerns, while appreciated, were unnecessary. I'd done nothing wrong. Besides, James was Professor Booker's assistant. I didn't like him—I didn't.

You're in trouble!

I pressed my lips together and took a deep, even breath as I followed Miss Witherstine out of the windmill. We tramped across the barren wheat fields, our shoes sticking into the dirt and grime. More than once, I had to struggle as my boot caught in a particularly damp bit of mud. More than once I thought about making a run for it.

I focused on Miss Witherstine's back. I watched her shoulders, rigid and straight, as we made it to Professor Booker's garden. The tense silence of Miss Witherstine seemed almost amplified by the crunching of our boots over the gravel pathway. We came around to the front of the house, and I paused as Miss Witherstine walked directly toward the stone archway and the gate. I hesitated, glancing back to Professor Booker's home, then quickened my step and followed.

Miss Witherstine was already in the carriage when I arrived. Her face flushed, she stared pointedly out the glass window opposite the door. The driver stared straight ahead, lips pressed together as I approached. Quietly, I stepped inside.

"Lillian, dear," Miss Witherstine shifted on the plush bench inside the carriage. I sat opposite her. I heard the driver snap the reigns and seconds later the carriage jerked as we set off down the main lane back toward Creekstone Manor. She smoothed out her skirt. "I think it's time you and I had a bit of a heart-to-heart, so to speak. A chat about womanhood."

I felt my stomach drop.

"You see," Miss Witherstine continued, "I find that Johnathon and I agree on almost everything. Everything that is, except you, my dear. Now, Johnathon is not known for…shall we say, meeting the status quo of high-societal life. His expectations for your upbringing are quite lacking, child."

"Lacking?" I asked and I felt my eye twitch. This was not how I thought our conversation would go. "In what way?"

Miss Witherstine pressed her lips together. "Precisely what I'm touching on. Such a haughty tone, darling. I fear for your *social* intelligence as much as Professor Booker fears for your *intellectual* intelligence, or mechanical abilities or—whatever it is he has you do in that dusty old workshop of his."

I swallowed. Did Professor Booker fear for my intelligence?

Of course—you're worthless. Why wouldn't he be worried about that?

Miss Witherstine continued, "It's high time you started to

behave like a lady, and as the only woman in your life it's my job to set the example in which you should follow."

I leaned forward and held the skirt of my dress in two balled fists. "Miss Witherstine, if this is about me leaving your party, I meant no disrespect—"

"First things first," Miss Witherstine barreled on, "you mustn't participate in traveling to the quarry—Johnathon should hardly be down there, let alone a lady like yourself. I've told him many times, I said, 'Johnathon, I don't care what you've found in the quarry. Sometimes you need to leave good enough alone,' but you know men."

"Miss Witherstine, the beasts are hardly a big enough obstacle to stop *either* of us from exploring whatever undiscovered science is down there!" I interjected.

"Evil lurks in the quarry, Lillian. I'll tell you, as I've told Johnathon, I will not fund any sort of experimentation on anything that he finds there. I fund his science, not magic."

"Professor Booker said it's not magic," I grumbled. As Professor Booker's benefactor, she was privileged to know every single thing Professor Booker worked on. I thought it was unnecessary and stupid to include her in things she clearly didn't understand.

Miss Witherstine continued, "Secondly, you shall not associate alone with James Cordington—or *any* male your age—in such a private location. You heard just today that harlots are not welcome here in Kesterfield. Now, if he were to ask to court you and you said yes—"

I felt heat rush to my cheeks and whatever sort of arguments I'd previously thought of fled my brain.

"Never in a million years!" I shouted. Miss Witherstine

finally paused, her mouth parted and her eyes wide. I sucked in a breath.

"We will continue this conversation when you've had a moment to calm yourself, Lillian." Miss Witherstine narrowed her eyes. "When we arrive, you're to go straight to the library and sequester yourself there until supper. Is that understood?"

"I had chores Professor Booker assigned to me," I tried to salvage the conversation, though I could feel my heart still hammering behind my ribs. "I wasn't there to be alone with a boy, least of all James Cordington!"

"Is that understood?" Miss Witherstine repeated. I frowned and leaned back, arms crossed.

"Yes," I snapped. I looked out the window, and we sat in silence, my stomach churning.

When we had arrived back at the manor, it seemed the tea had been concluded—the guests and their carriages had gone. The maids and servants were halfway through removing the decorations when I walked through the grand oak doors for the second time that day.

I bit my tongue and silently moved to the left wing of the house, where I knew the library was stationed. It was small in comparison to Professor Booker's, and filled with educational books on habit and society. I found one titled *History of The Beasts*. Unfortunately, it contained no history, but instead told of all the people the beasts had gobbled up. After a few hours of suffering through the book, I was called for dinner.

We sat in her large dining room, Miss Witherstine on one end, and Iris and I at the other. My chair had been shoved next to Iris's, and though they were evenly spaced, our elbows occasionally brushed each other if we weren't careful.

"You know, Lillian, I was thinking," Miss Witherstine spoke from the other side of the table. I froze, spoon halfway to my mouth. Iris continued to eat. Miss Witherstine didn't look up from her soup as she continued, "I have this plan, you see. Johnathon is, of course, out of town until next week. As a surprise, I was going to host him a party when he came back into town. A townwide affair, really. It's just that…well, ever since you've come to stay with him, I've not had quality time with the man. You know, we used to have weekly afternoon tea together. But Johnathon is terribly busy, as I'm sure you're aware. I'm not quite sure I know what he even likes anymore! And, well, I was thinking…"

She set the spoon down and finally looked up at me. "You, as his *niece*, should assist me!"

I glanced over at Iris. She sipped the soup from her spoon delicately, which I found fascinating, for soup was very hard to eat delicately. Even Professor Booker couldn't do it. He always slurped his from a large wooden spoon that had a small crack so that whenever he brought it to his mouth, it would drip a small drop of soup onto his shirt. Slowly, I turned back to Miss Witherstine.

"How long did you think about this, Miss Witherstine?"

"Please," Miss Witherstine smiled, though her eyes remained cold. "Call me Victoria."

I smoothed out the napkin on my lap. "Of course…Victoria, you see…I just—I've not been one for social gatherings. I'd much rather continue working on my inventions if you don't mind. Parties seem to be more in line with *your* skill set."

"Oh, no! Nonsense," Miss Witherstine waved her hand. "You see, I need your help! This would mean so much to

31

your uncle—if he saw you, his niece, rising to the occasion."

I opened my mouth to argue when I thought of the letter.

What had been Professor Booker's first rule?

You must obey Miss Witherstine.

I shut it again.

"Are we in agreement?" Miss Witherstine asked as she moved her fork back into place on the table. I suppressed the rising pressure in my stomach and gave a quiet, prim nod. I would obey Professor Booker by obeying Miss Witherstine, finish the dragon, and figure out our next steps to the stones—all before he got back! I could do it. I had to. Miss Witherstine grinned. "Oh, good. I'll send for a week's worth of your belongings to be retrieved and brought here. After all, Johnathon did ask me to keep an eye on you, and party planning is so time-consuming, so we kill two birds with one stone, so to speak."

She broke off her sentence with a laugh. My shoulders dropped, and I stood, my chair scrapping against the wooden floor. "Wait—I never agreed to—"

"After all, we don't want you traveling so much through the forest. What with the beasts about. Besides, you, alone, in that big empty house. People could *talk*, and we certainly want none of that."

My stomach dropped. "But—I've important work to do—"

"And I'm sure James Cordington, Johnathon's *original* assistant, can and will be most gracious in handling those arrangements while you stay with us." Miss Witherstine waved a hand. "You can both be excused from the table. Lillian, a maid will show you to the guest bedroom."

Iris stood, thanked Miss Witherstine for the meal, and vanished through the side door to the dining room. My cheeks felt hot, and the room was suddenly stuffy. I briskly stormed from the dining room. From the corner of my eye, I caught Miss Witherstine smiling as she brought her spoon to her lips.

"This way," a maid stood at the ready outside the room. Slowly, she led me up the large staircase and to the right. My fists shook as we traveled through the house and came to a large guest bedroom. I stepped inside, and the maid shut the door behind me. I listened to her footsteps retreat, then stormed over to the window. It overlooked the perfect gardens of Creekstone Manor.

I never liked staying in a new place. The first three weeks that I'd moved in with the Professor had been hell for both of us as we adjusted to each other's…eccentricities. It was only after he'd allowed me into his workshop and started to teach me the fundamentals of his craft that we began to understand one another.

He was a busy man. I wouldn't pretend that him taking the time out of his day to teach me, let alone include me in his future experiments on the stones, didn't mean the world to me. How could I prove that to him while I was stuck in Creekstone Manor?

"Stay here?" I whispered under my breath as I began to pace. "Stay here?"

My face screwed together, and a deep pressure threatened to build inside of me. I reached up and tugged on my two braids.

It's what you deserve.

"No!" I hissed and turned on my heel as I continued to pace.

Liars deserve punishment.

"No…" I whispered. I came to the curtain and huffed before spinning around once more. "No, I haven't lied—"

Your duty is to keep Professor Booker's secrets. To be a good apprentice.

This is your fault.

I faltered…perhaps this insidious whisper had a point…

The door clicked open, and I spun around. Iris slipped inside and eased the large white door shut behind her. She looked at me, her eyes narrowing.

"Now you've done it," she said.

"Done what?" I huffed. Iris rolled her eyes.

"Angered Miss Witherstine. She'll be in a terrible mood all week." Iris floated into the room, her skirt fluttering around her delicate feet. She moved toward the four-poster bed and wrapped an arm around one of the posts. She spun to face me. I leaned against the window, my arms crossed.

"My, you really don't know how to control your face, do you?" Iris clicked her tongue. "Well, I did try to warn you. It's not my fault you didn't catch the hint."

"The hint?" I asked. "What hint could you have possibly given me to warn me of *this* specific outcome?"

Iris blinked. "At the party. Don't you remember?"

I frowned. For the first time since I'd been introduced to the girl, I saw a flash of irritation contort her pretty features.

"You were practically scowling," she continued, raising her eyebrows as she searched my face. She clicked her tongue again and sat on the edge of the bed. "I said to you 'you should smile—'"

"How is *that* a warning that Miss Witherstine would kidnap me?" It was my turn to look irritated.

Iris shook her head. "It's *not* a kidnapping. I'm sure you'll be returned to your uncle at the end of the week."

"Professor Booker left me specific instructions. I've important tasks that need—"

"And surely," Iris stood, "You would know which of the two of the parental figures we're discussing is more dangerous when angered."

I bit my tongue. "You've not seen Professor Booker upset."

"And you've not seen Miss Witherstine cross." Iris bit back. She shook her head. "You really think you're in no danger?"

"Oh, what danger does Miss Witherstine pose except passive-aggressive scheming?"

Iris stood. I watched as she walked toward me, her fists clenched at her side. She stopped right at my side, facing the window.

"What are you doing?" I asked. Iris tilted her head to the side.

"Oh, good evening, Miss Cordington," Iris mimicked the airy tone of Miss Witherstine to such perfection that I actually glanced toward the door to make sure we were still alone. Iris shifted, glaring at me from the corner of her eyes. "Oh, yes, and how *is* James doing? I hear he spends an awful lot of time up at Professor Booker's home with that niece of his, Lillian... What do you think of Lillian? Well, I think she's a fine girl, really, if not on the odd side, but...well, no, I shouldn't say..."

I swallowed as Iris tapped her chin.

"Well, Miss Cordington, if you can really keep a secret..." Iris turned her voice down to a whisper. "I just...I know Professor Booker *said* she was his niece, but—"

My heart suddenly hammered in my ears. I felt the color drain from my face as Iris shifted to stare directly at me.

"If he were really her uncle, wouldn't she call him that instead of constantly referring to him as 'Professor'?" Iris smiled.

"He is my uncle," I whispered as Iris rolled her eyes. I stepped toward her. "He is!"

"The point, my dear Lillian…" Iris swept away from the window and toward the large white doors. She rested a hand on the silver knob and glanced at me from over her shoulder. Her hair swept along her back, and her eyelashes batted against her cheeks. "Is that Miss Witherstine has more power than you have given her credit for, and she's not above weaving falsehoods. You've more than your own reputation at stake. Were there a scandal about, well…Miss Witherstine would have no choice but to remove herself as a benefactor of his inventions, and then where would you be?"

And with that, she swept out of the room.

IT HAD BEEN JUST THREE days since I'd been coerced to stay in the dreaded manor Miss Witherstine and Iris called a home. Quickly, I learned the rules of society. I had to be present and presentable during all the meals, and any free time I had was quickly squandered away with preparations for the *stupid* party.

I spent hours choosing colors, streamers, flower arrangements, food items, and more. Well...I say "choose"...

"Which napkin do you think we should set out?" Miss Witherstine asked. "We have an eggshell and a cream."

I looked up from the notepad I'd nabbed. My fountain pen had a small crack at the nib, so the ink splotched as I detailed all the changes I still had to make on the dragon. I tilted the pen up, away from the paper, to keep the ink from smearing everywhere.

"Eggshell should be fine," I stated. Miss Witherstine gave a light hum and held up both napkins.

"Now, you haven't even looked, Lillian. Look closely. Which do you think Johnathon would prefer?"

I set the notepad in my lap, my lips pursed. I felt my right eye begin to twitch. Iris sat in the corner of the room, sewing. We had not spoken a single word to each other since our previous…conversation. I looked at both the napkins and then at Miss Witherstine.

"He wouldn't have a preference," I stated. Then, at Miss Witherstine's tight smile, said, "*Eggshell*."

Miss Witherstine scooted forward and held them closer. I suppressed any and all rage that threatened to explode within me and changed my answer. "The cream, then?"

"Oh, what a wonderful choice!" Miss Witherstine exclaimed. "I do say, you're getting better and better at this party planning the more you do it. In no time, you'll be throwing bashes like these completely on your own! A respectable young lady that will bring such pride to Kesterfield!"

By Wednesday around midafternoon, I'd made so many "not-decisions" that I felt nauseous. The room around me had grown hot and stuffy. I pressed my wrist against my forehead and took a deep breath. Miss Witherstine continued to fold napkins, unaware of my discomfort. I grit my teeth and looked down at my lap.

You won't achieve anything in your life if you stay here. You're being lazy.

I shot a glance to Iris, her focus on her sewing. I snuck a look toward Miss Witherstine, who had busied herself with arranging a vase of flowers. I looked back down at my pen, moved the nib to my skirt, and pressed down. I watched as the fabric began to soak up the ink, a big black stain against the light blue skirt.

"Oh," I gasped and stood up. "Oh no! I've spilled ink on my skirt."

Miss Witherstine and Iris looked up at the same time. Iris narrowed her eyes as I curtsied.

"Please, *Victoria*, excuse me while I go clean myself up."

And then I was rushing out the door, down the hall, and out of Creekstone Manor. I ran past the front gate, took a right, and rushed across the back fields of Kesterfield toward Professor Booker's house.

I fled through the gate. James was tending the garden and suddenly stood. I stopped.

"Lillian? Are you—" James dusted the dirt off his hands. I quickly turned toward the workshop, my heart hammering in my ears.

"I have work to do—experiments and such. *Don't you dare bother me!*" I rushed off toward the windmill that loomed on the edge of Professor Booker's property. My breath came in sharp and ragged as I stormed across the barren fields. I felt my arms tingle as I slammed open the wooden door and let it crash behind me. I closed my eyes, taking in the familiar smell of metal and oil. My face still felt hot and sweat stuck to my hairline. I smoothed my palms on my skirt and opened my eyes. Things were not as I had left them in the workshop.

The Professor's inventions had been moved around. The piles of scrap metal were tidied up, and the floor was freshly swept and mopped. I quickly looked at Professor Booker's bookcase—and let out a breath as I spotted the stones still in their original places. I sniffed and slowly walked toward the workbench.

My dragon sat on the same wooden workbench, though it had been pushed to the back of the table. In front of it was a large feather duster machine that had broken some time ago.

I'd been meaning to fix it for ages. It stood on a set of four wheels, propelled by tiny bursts of steam. Its body was a large, rotating cylinder with wiggling metallic arms, feather dusters attached to the ends. Professor Booker lovingly referred to it as "Dust-In."

I looked past it to the dragon. Its jaw still got stuck when it was supposed to open. The wings seemed to me a tacky addition—a last-minute choice on my part. The tail was too sharp, and the claws needed to be buffed, chiseled down, and rounded out. The eyes had oil smeared on them. I bit my tongue and felt a pressure begin to build behind my eyes.

Useless. Weak. Worthless.

I felt my lip quiver, and I quickly bit down on it. Professor Booker was scheduled to return Sunday morning.

You'll never finish it in time. He will be disappointed in you.

"I can do it." I wiped my nose and grabbed the wrench on the table. "I can. I'm not pitiful, I will be a great inventor, I—"

I heard the door open and I froze.

"Lilly?" James asked.

I sniffed and continued to work on the dragon in front of me. He tried again.

"Lil—"

"What?" I snapped and immediately regretted it. With my lips pulled tight, I slowly turned to look at him.

James stood there, his lips pulled back into a thin line, the usual smirk gone, his arms crossed as he leaned against the door frame. "Are you okay?"

I pushed myself away from the dragon and smoothed down my skirt. I pressed down the lump in my throat, blinking away the sudden moisture in my eyes, and said, "Yes, I'm fine.

Thank you for retrieving Dust-In from the house—I'll fix it right now so you may keep tending the garden."

James nodded slowly. I walked over to the peg on the wall and grabbed my leather apron and gloves.

James cleared his throat.

I ignored him and walked briskly past him back toward Dust-In. I opened a metal door in Dust-In's cylinder body and pushed up my sleeves. Inside the cylinder was a mess of tubes and metal pipes. The gears were stuck—dust, ironically, had clogged them.

"You lyin'?" James asked from behind me.

"James, I've said I'm busy," I huffed as I craned my neck to look over my shoulder.

"You didn't answer the question," James's voice rumbled as he spoke, quiet and calm. I pressed my lips together and turned back to Dust-In.

He mocks you. He'll take joy in your pain. He really is the better apprentice.

"*No*," I muttered with a shake of my head, reaching forward to grab a cracked tube. Oil dripped from the hole.

"You *are* lying?" James stepped forward. I grit my teeth.

"No!" I snapped as I used the wrench to wrestle with the nut at the end of the tube. I yanked, but it wouldn't budge.

"You're not lying?" James took another step forward.

"James—"

"Are you okay, or are you *not* okay? It's a simple question."

"I really don't have time—"

I jumped as my wrench gave way, the nut finally loosening. My wrench slipped and connected with the tube. Oil spurted from the hole and onto my blouse. I looked down at my shirt and slowly, I turned around to James, my teeth clenched. He faltered.

"I…" He shrugged helplessly as he motioned to me.

I felt my nostrils begin to flare. My face was hot and my neck itched.

He crossed his arms and looked at the ground. "You're just brushing me off. Professor Booker told me to help out in here while he's gone, so I'm just trying to see what I can do."

Ha! You thought he was here for you. He's just doing his duty. He doesn't care about you.

My heart quickened and my eyes widened. I quickly spun around to face the machine.

"I don't need your help," I huffed.

James chuckled. "He said you'd say that."

"Well, then I don't—"

"And he said you'd say that too."

Suddenly, his hand was on my shoulder, and he was so very close to me, and all I could think of was Miss Witherstine bursting in at this moment—the things she'd say, that she'd think—and I jumped away. My back cracked against the machine. I heard a click and whirled around. Inside Dust-In, I watched as the gears began to whine and shift. The arms began to rotate, slowly at first. The tubes twisted inside, and oil continued to sputter out. A dial turned to red and steam began to spill from loose crevices and cracks.

"Oh! James—look what you did! It's a mess—" A stray arm from the duster whirled through the air and struck my cheek. I stumbled away with a gasp. Dust-In wriggled, the open metal flap on his cylinder body clanging shut as he began to spin.

James lurched in front of me. I held my face with my hand and took a step away as James and the machine began to wrestle.

The machine let out a high-pitched whine as it spun faster and faster. James gasped as the arms wriggled in the air. He grabbed hold, and suddenly, it was out of its stand and twirling on the ground like a spinning top. Metal smacked against flesh, and James stumbled back next to me.

"Yikes—" he huffed. I looked up. The machine spun and whirred directly toward Professor Booker's bookshelf.

"James—" I hit his arm and took half a step forward. Dust-In whirled closer and closer to the bookshelf. "James—*Professor Booker's stuff! The—the stones!*"

James scrambled to his feet and grabbed a discarded pipe. He ran toward the machine, battling its arms as they swung toward him like an elaborate fencing match.

"No!" the shriek erupted from my mouth as I saw the metal arm swing toward Professor Booker's bookshelf. It connected with the glass pane, shattering it upon impact. I grabbed each of the ends of my braids and tugged as I watched. The turquoise stone bobbed lazily in the air and away from the shelf. James heaved the metal pipe through the air and landed a solid hit on Dust-In's middle. It whined, and steam hissed from its joints. The metal arms flailed wildly around and cracked into the bookcase again.

Books and pages erupted from the bookshelves and clattered to the ground. The other stones rolled. The ice-white stone bounced off a half-open drawer and tumbled inside it. The other two missed the drawer and clattered to the ground. They rolled past the machine and James.

Dust-In bumped into the shelf once, twice, three times, and then spun back toward James. He jogged backward, eyes trained on the out-of-control machine. My eyes darted to the ground and I watched as James's boot came down on the purple stone.

Violet light erupted from under his feet and lit up the entire workshop. I held up my hands and shielded my eyes from the vibrant purple hues. Something rubbed against my boot, and I shrieked, jumping away.

"Oh my—" I gasped. Vines sprouted from the cracks in between the stone floor of the workshop. They wound up from the ground, sprouting and budding as they came to life.

"Lillian—*help!*" James hobbled on one foot, holding the foot that had crunched on the stone. It almost seemed to have turned into a cannon, greenery and leaves shooting from the bottom of his boot and snaking across the floor of the workshop. I watched as they embraced Dust-In. He whined as he strained against nature.

James tugged his boot off and hurled it across the room. I looked back down to the ground and gasped. The vines had begun to grow over my feet. I tugged my boots away and scrambled toward the workbench. I clambered on top, next to the dragon. The whole building shuddered as the massive vines clustered among the inner workings of the windmill. A thick, coiling stem grew up and around the furnace in the middle of the room. I heard a crack of wood and looked above me.

Vines and leaves grew from the ceiling and intertwined with the vines that had grown up from the floor and spread along the walls. James hopped onto the table next to me.

"What the—"

"Shh!" I held my finger against his lips and stared at the workshop around me. It seemed as though, in a matter of seconds, ages had passed. The chaos of nature clashed with the metallic inventions and machinery in the room. The purple light faded, and the soft yellow of sunbeams through the circular windows on the wall once again washed over the room. Slowly, I looked over toward Dust-In.

The machine groaned—steam hissed from its cracks. The green vines that had tangled up and around Dust-In grew dark with oil stains. His head shuddered and clicked, straining to spin. Nature and machine caught in a war. I held my breath and scanned the workshop for the missing stones. A flash of turquoise caught my eye, and I watched as the blue stone twirled in the air. It spun in a small circle, just four feet off the ground. I searched the ground for the red or icy-white stones but couldn't catch sight of them. I was sure they had been completely buried beneath the jungle floor that had spread across the workshop.

"Lillian—" James pointed at the turquoise stone, which had spun lazily just in front of Dust-In. I heard a snap and watched as Dust-In broke free and fell forward with a deep, painful groan of metal.

An object at rest remains at rest, and an object in motion remains in motion at a constant speed and in a straight line unless acted on by an unbalanced force. Every object in the universe obeyed this rule, and the turquoise rock was no different.

Dust-In's arms broke free and flailed in the air once more. It smacked into the stone, which shot across the room with a whine. I snapped my neck to the side as I followed its flight.

Secondly, the acceleration of an object depends on the mass

of the object and the amount of force applied. Perhaps if Dust-In had not hit the stone with such ferocity, and if the stone were heavier, we would have been fine.

But Dust-In had smacked the stone as hard as he could—and the stone was small and lightweight, so our fate was decided. I could do nothing as the stone met the wall of the windmill and shattered. A blinding blue light shot out. I winced but forced my eyes to remain open.

Thirdly, whenever one object exerts a force on another object, the second object exerts an equal and opposite on the first.

Whatever science controlled the stones adhered to this rule as well, I was sure. For it exerted an incomprehensible amount of force on everything inside the workshop as a reaction to being so rudely shattered.

My mouth dropped open as everything in the workshop began to float.

My braids floated up past my chin. My skirt fluttered around my knees. I scrambled in the air, a foot off the ground, and grabbed onto the metallic dragon.

"Lillian!" James screamed. "What is happening?!"

He had drifted off to the left and tumbled, head over foot, just above Dust-In. The machine churned into the plant life underneath it as it continued to spin and tumble on the ground. James's arms pinwheeled as he tried to stay upright.

"Stay calm!" I shouted. "Oh—crackers!"

My skirt fluttered in the air. My stomach lurched as everything began to spin to the right. The wood of the tables and bookcases creaked as they turned. My heart hammered in my throat. My hands grew cold. I gripped the dragon's metal wings as I sat atop it, my braids flying in the air above my shoulders.

We spun faster and faster. I think I started screaming at one point as everything began to blur around me. And just as fast as it started, suddenly, whatever had grabbed us and spun us let go. I yelped as we fell to the ground. Metal and wood crunched and crashed. James scrambled out of Dust-In's way as it shattered upon impact with the ground, the gears finally clicking to a stop. Oil bled from his mangled body and leaked in a thick pool on the ground.

I heard a deep crunch and finally found the red stone as my dragon and I landed on it. The third broken stone gave off a deep red glow, quickly filling the workshop with ruby red light. I scrambled off the dragon and landed sharply on the mix of broken debris, ivy, and ancient rock. I hissed as I scraped my hands on the floor. I looked down—cuts marred my palms. I shot up and tried to run for the door. The ground shook, and I stumbled against the wooden workbench.

"Lillian!"

I looked behind me and hastily bushed my braids out of my face. James had his back pressed against the wall, his face cast in a deep, blood-red light. He pointed a single, trembling finger toward the middle of the room. The ground shook again. I looked toward the dragon.

The red from the rock glowed and crept up into the brass.

The metal claw twitched. I took a sharp breath.

I watched as my dragon's claw curled around the pieces of rock, and the sound of a heartbeat began to reverberate through the air.

My hands shot over my mouth, and I scrambled away. My back smacked against the wall.

I watched as the metallic wings flexed out. The gears

chittered as the beast cocked its head to the side. The marbles in my dragon's eyes began to glow. Slowly, it lifted its paw with the shattered, broken pieces of the stone and shoved it fully in its mouth. I watched as the stones shifted through the metal teeth and collected in the back of its throat. The light in the room faded, the red seeping back toward the dragon, and everything around me went still.

My head swam as I sat, still as a statue, staring at the machine. It was moving. How was it moving? I brought my legs up to my chest. Across the workshop, James stood cautiously and then darted toward me. He tripped over broken metal and splintered wood and then sat, in a heap, next to me.

"Lillian—look at me," he whispered as he grabbed my hands. He lifted my chin toward him, his eyes searching mine. "Are you alright? Are you hurt?"

I numbly shook my head. I heard the clicking of gears and looked past him.

The dragon stood, crouched like a lion, ready to pounce. Its glowing, unmoving marble eyes locked dead and center on me. I sucked in a sharp breath and squeezed James's hand. He turned and then dropped low to the ground. He held out his arms in front of me, shielding me. I looked down at my palms, the red dust from the stone mixing with the beads of blood oozing from the scrapes in my hands.

Metal shifted and clicked. I looked up. The dragon's tail flicked behind it as it eased down into a deeper crouch.

"It's…" I whispered. "I…"

"*Lillian*," James hissed through tight lips. The dragon unhinged its jaw. My gut dropped. A click came from the back of its throat. The inside of its maw lit as a flame caught the spark. James grabbed my hand, and we ran.

WE TORE OUT OF THE WINDMILL. I felt a burst of heat at my heels and risked a hurried glance behind us. Fire billowed from the door of the workshop. I gasped. James ran in front of me, his hand clamped around my wrist as he all but pulled me forward. My heart hammered in my throat and I put on a burst of speed. Behind me, I could hear the clanking of shifting metal.

"The forest—" James called. "We'll lose it in the forest!"

We leapt through the garden—not bothering to go around the Professor's vegetables and strawberry bushes. I stumbled over a weed and clutched James's sleeve. He grunted, pulled me up, and we kept running. I risked another look behind us. The dragon bounded after us like a wolf chasing its prey. My heart lurched into my throat.

We tore through the gate, past the walls, and onto the dirt path.

My hands stung. My head spun.

"Oh, crackers," I hissed.

The stones were gone. Professor Booker had worked so hard to excavate them—they were *gone*! I sucked in a breath as we leaped over a fallen tree. James slipped his hand from my wrist to grip my hand instead. I winced as my palm stung but found my eyes locked on our intertwined fingers. I looked up to James. He kept his eyes forward as he led us through the forest. Behind us, I heard the crunching of twigs and leaves.

The stones had side effects one couldn't have possibly dreamed of! This could be an undiscovered side of science the world had never before seen—or perhaps one that had been lost to us through time. I'd been there—I'd seen what had happened! I could write about it and—

"Oh, *crackers!*" I shrieked. The ground beneath us tilted off into a steep hill. My boot slipped in a patch of mud. I squeezed my eyes shut and felt James's strong arms wrap tightly around my head. We fell, rolling down the steep hill. I grit my teeth as stones and sticks bit into my back. The world spun faster and faster until, finally, we came to a stop.

I opened my eyes. We'd landed in a soft patch of grass. It was a miracle we hadn't hit a tree on the way down the hill. I shifted and looked underneath me at James. His face was twisted into a grimace, his eyes screwed shut, his arms still wrapped tight around my body. My tongue suddenly felt swollen in my mouth, my eyes wide, our faces only four inches apart. I stayed frozen as he sucked in breath after breath, his chest rising and falling under my hands.

A twig snapped, and I looked at the top of the hill. The dragon stared down from between two thick bushes, its glowing marble eyes fixing onto us. I held my breath as I stared at it. My dragon...moving on its own! Smoke trailed lazily from the side of its mouth. Then, slowly, it stepped back and disappeared into the foliage. I sat up and scrambled off of James. Sunlight trickled from between the leaves of the forest around us.

"*James!*" I hissed. My braids had come undone in the tumble and my hair stuck to my cheeks. I swiped at the wisps and struggled to my feet. "James!"

"What?" he groaned and folded into a fetal position. "*Oh, my ribs—*"

"James—it's alive! Did you see it—hear it? It's alive! It's—it's alive!" I stumbled a step away, my hands tangled in my thick strands of hair. My heart hammered in its cage, and for a brief, babbling moment, all I could do was shout "it's alive" over and over.

"Lillian—Lillian, shut up!" James sat with a groan. "It's alive and it was trying *to kill us!*"

I slid to the ground next to him. "But James—it could move! The legs worked, and it had eyes, and it looked as though it could see us! Don't you see what this means?!"

James numbly shook his head.

"Think, James!" I hissed. "There wasn't any explaining with science what happened in there—it was *magic!* Pure and simple as that. And now we are faced with the extraordinary opportunity of learning to understand it! Oh! Just wait until Professor—"

I snapped my mouth shut. What *would* Professor Booker say?

"Understand it? It was chasing us!" James shook his head. His hair was disheveled, and mud caked his chin. It was then I realized how close the two of us sat. My hand rested next to his in the mud, the tips of our fingers touching. I scrambled to my feet and prayed that my flaming face was covered in mud, and pretended to search the hill above us for the beast.

I looked down at my skirt. Torn and muddy—I could imagine Miss Witherstine fainting at the sight.

"Come along," I spoke crisply as I hiked up the hill. "We have to find the dragon before it goes into town."

"Lillian—"

I barreled forward past trees and bushes. James stalked behind me. My eyes trailed along the ground, searching for any sign of brass or metal. I burst out of the forest through a thicket of leaves and stumbled to a stop in front of a small creek. It shimmered as it gurgled along the smooth stones.

"Lillian."

I kept my eyes firmly ahead and quickly stepped along the bank of the creek. I searched the water to see if there was a dry section of rocks to step on—or at least a section shallower than the rest.

"Lillian, would you just look at me?" James snapped.

I turned, arms crossed tight over my chest. With my jaw clenched and my eyes half-open, I made a point of looking at his feet—one shoe missing, both appendages covered in mud—up his legs—his knee was bleeding—his shirt, and then, finally, his face. I slowly raised my eyebrows as I stared into his honey-brown eyes. He sucked in a small breath and smoothed a scraped hand over his tussled hair.

"Lilly—I don't know what's going on!" He dragged his hand over his face. I felt my shoulders fall, and every ounce of defensive pride blew out like a candle.

"I know—James, I'm..." I bit my lip. Failure was not an option. With all four stones gone and now a magical mechanical dragon on the loose, it was becoming more and more likely that Professor Booker would come home to a disaster rather than a townwide party in his honor. Besides…I knew what happened to the inventions that didn't work out.

Professor Booker would work relentlessly, day and night, on his machines. But sometimes, even geniuses like the Professor couldn't fix something. Sometimes, that thing was just too broken at the start of the journey to be fixed.

I'd watched the Professor grumble under his breath, face red and scrunched together, as he'd pull whatever invention he'd given up on all the way over the stone steps and into the attic where it would sit, forever collecting dust. Away from his sight so he would not be reminded of his failings. Up in a corner of the attic, next to me and my workbench.

I would not let my dragon be discarded like one of his failed inventions.

I pressed my tongue against the back of my teeth and squeezed my forearms with my hands.

"James," I whispered and I shut my eyes. "I'm going to, one day, be a brilliant inventor. This…this is my opportunity! Don't you see that?"

James took a breath. He stepped toward me, clapped his hands together and leaned forward.

"Right…what do you need me to do?"

I blinked. "What?"

"Professor Booker gave me a letter asking me to specifically help you out this week. So, what do you need me to do?" he asked.

"A letter? What did it say?" My mind stuttered as I imagined what Professor Booker had to say about *me* to James. I watched as James straightened. He scratched the back of his head and looked up at the sky.

"It, uh…doesn't matter," he shrugged. Then, he looked back at me, and my heart skipped a beat. "Lillian Booker. What do you need me to do?"

I felt a grin poke at my lips. My brain felt like someone had attached Professor Booker's lightning machine to it. So many possibilities lay before me. Discoveries and science. A bright new world at the tips of my fingers. I let my hands drop to my sides and whirled back toward the river.

"Despite the fact that the dragon chased us here into the forest, we must find it," I said as I stepped across the river. I heard James's foot splash into the water behind me as he followed. I stepped onto the bank on the opposite side and turned to him.

"Okay." James smoothed his hands over his trousers. "How do we do that without it eating us?"

I scrunched my nose. "It's a machine, James Cordington. Machines don't eat."

"Yeah, and they also don't come alive and chase you." James rolled his eyes. I had opened my mouth for a retort when I heard a snap of a twig. I looked toward the forest, eyes narrowed, as James continued to prattle on.

"We've no idea what this thing is capable of—it very well could eat. Humans, might I add—"

"Shh!" I held up a hand. "Did you hear that?"

James blinked and looked toward the forest. "No, I was—"

"Shh!"

We both fell silent and slowly edged toward the trees. A nearby bush shook, the branches and leaves dancing. I held my breath, and James took a quiet step in front of me. Something shiny caught my eye, darting between two leaves.

"There—" I pointed and watched as the bush shook and the creature slipped away. "James—it was right there!"

I took off, scrambling around the bush and running once more through the forest.

I SURGED THROUGH THE FOREST, my feet traveling lightly over the grass and mud.

"Lillian—" James cut himself off with a curse as a branch smacked him in the face.

I sped past trees and under low-hanging branches. Behind me, I could hear James struggling through the brush. I ducked under a particularly large branch and heard a small thunk.

"Jiminy cricket!" James shouted. "Lillian—would you slow down?"

I paused only as I reached the edge of the forest. Before us was a dirt path, and beyond that were the sweeping farm-lands of Kesterfield. I leaned against a tree and realized my breaths were coming in ragged and desperate gasps. Sweat caked my forehead, and I wiped my brow with a torn sleeve of my blouse. James came up next to me. He rested his hands on his knees, his head hanging forward. I avoided looking at his collar, the shirt torn and open.

"James—do you see it?" I asked, peering around the forest. "Do you think anyone else saw?"

The distant sound of hooves and the whining roll of a wagon's wheels came from our right. I looked down the path, watching the bend in the road. A black horse appeared and I ducked to the ground. James continued to breathe heavily next to me, and with a scowl, I grabbed his sleeve and tugged him to the ground. He grunted as he stumbled onto the forest floor. I watched as the horse pulled a bright and richly decorated carriage up the hill and toward Professor Booker's home. I narrowed my eyes. Now, where had I seen that carriage before…

"Oh, *crackers!*" I slapped a hand over my cheek. "Oh—oh, James, oh my—it's—"

"What? The dragon?" James whispered.

"*Miss Witherstine!*" I shook his shoulder. "It's Miss Witherstine's carriage!"

James and I watched as the carriage traveled over the dirt path and around the hill. I sucked in a breath. James and I looked at each other and, at the same time, cried, "*the workshop!*"

I scrambled to my feet and took off over the grassy fields. James overtook me within seconds, running ahead. He jumped onto the stone wall and vanished on the other side. I struggled up and over, hesitating at the top to look around. No sign of my dragon. A part of my brain wondered if we'd made up the entire thrilling experience. I pushed it aside and slid off the other side of the wall.

Miss Witherstine would be at the house in a matter of moments. I had work to do. I took off toward the house and slipped in through the back door into the kitchen. Flies had begun to gather on the dishes along the sink.

"*Oh—*" I swatted at them and tore through the door and

into the hallway. I rushed up the steps in the entryway, tripping over papers. They scattered in the air and fluttered down the stairs behind me as I tore up the steps and down the hall toward my bedroom. I flung off my skirt, wrestled off my blouse, and dropped them in the hallway. I slid into my bedroom and took a glance at myself in the mirror. Stained and dirty underclothes, with mud caking my chin. I grabbed a spare blouse and skirt from my dresser and wrestled them over my head. Then I quickly collected my hair and tied it back into a bun.

"Lillian!" I heard James cry from downstairs—the front door squeaking loudly as he eased it shut. I grabbed a cloth and dipped it in the water basin at my vanity table. Quickly, I scrubbed my chin and any other dirt splotches I could see. James continued to call from downstairs. "Lillian—*where are you?* She's coming to the gate!"

I tripped over the clothes discarded on the ground and grabbed a spare belt. Quickly, I wrapped it around my waist and, with a deep breath, smoothed my skirt.

"James—start cleaning up the kitchen," I called from the top of the stairs.

"What?!" he yelped.

"Quickly—grab dishes and start scrubbing!" I yelled. "And for the love of God, act natural!"

I heard James trip over something downstairs, curse, and then thunder into the kitchen. I paused at the top of the steps and took another breath.

It wasn't lying, I told myself as I descended the stairs. I could hear water sloshing from the kitchen basin. I paused at the bottom of the stairs, smoothing my hair behind my ears. *I wasn't lying...*

Three knocks resounded through the hallway.

"Coming!" I cried, then counted slowly to five before walking toward the door. "Oh, Miss Witherstine. Good afternoon. Is everything alright?"

Miss Witherstine pressed her lips tightly together. She looked over me, her eyes narrowing as she stared down at my frame.

"You didn't tell me where you went." She smoothed down her pink skirt with a delicate hand. "It's not...*right*...for a young lady such as yourself to go gallivanting off by herself... Let me guess...James Cordington is here?"

I pressed out a smile and bit down on my tongue. "He's doing the chores Professor Booker left for him. *I* was fixing a machine for Professor Booker as part of *my* chores."

Miss Witherstine hummed lightly and stepped around me, her eyes widening as she took in the space around us.

"My, my, my," she pursed her lips as she turned away from me and back toward the spiral staircase.

I followed her gaze and took a proper glance around the entryway. Wooden carved figures of animals sat in nearly every corner of the home. In all honesty, I didn't understand the Professor's obsession with such home decor. The carvings themselves were decent, though nothing that deserved special praise. In the entryway, a large birdlike creature—a crane, or so I'd been informed—sat towering behind piles of papers and journals. Coats and hats hung on its beak and the wings spread so far out into the walkway you had to duck just to get by.

Right across from it sat a beaver on top of a slim dresser. It faced the mirror on the wall, its beady eyes staring through the reflection and to wherever you happened to be in the room. Its tail had been broken in half once, and then glued back on, so now there was a thin white crack along the middle. In its hands, it held up a box that contained an assortment of small metal keys—the locks to which had long been lost.

"*Oh goodness, Johnathon,*" Miss Witherstine muttered. Then, she shook her head, took in a breath, and set off down the hall.

"Miss Witherstine—" I stalked after her, close behind. Her boots clicked against the floor, and with her shoulders held back and her nose held high, she turned into the kitchen.

James was at the sink, a scowl on his face, his hair pushed back by sweat and water, his sleeves rolled up over toned arms. I stared at him for a brief second, my heart fluttering, then shook myself and looked up at Miss Witherstine.

"Dishes?" she asked. James paused and glanced up.

"Oh, Miss Witherstine... Good afternoon." James wiped his brow, pushing more blond hair out of place. I glanced over the kitchen.

"He's supposed to clean the whole house for Professor Booker, you see," I explained. "He'll...probably be here all week *searching* for things to *clean.*"

I sent James a quick glance. He nodded in understanding.

Miss Witherstine clicked her tongue as her eyes scanned the kitchen. "Well, he won't have to search very long..."

"You can say that again," James muttered and turned back to the sink, shaking his head. "So *many* chores."

"James, you certainly have your work cut out for you," Miss Witherstine addressed him. She paused, eying his attire. "James, whatever happened to you?"

James's eyes widened as he quickly looked down at his outfit. He looked at me, then at Miss Witherstine.

"I get...really passionate about gardening. Must've left my boot in the uh...garden," he smiled, then quickly started to scrub a dish.

Miss Witherstine frowned, then nodded and turned toward me. "Come along, Lillian. You've not finished planning the party, and you promised you'd help."

I smoothed my skirt and nodded. "Of course. Goodbye, Mr. Cordington."

James scrunched his nose. "Bye, *Miss Booker*. Don't worry, I'll *search everywhere* for things to clean."

I gave a light curtsy, and then I followed Miss Witherstine out of the kitchen. I knew he would find the dragon while I was otherwise occupied. He was good like that.

We walked briskly toward the carriage and I found that, as Miss Witherstine lectured me, I didn't mind. In fact, I could barely pay her any attention... My mind was occupied with much bigger...brassier things.

THE SUN HAD SET HOURS AGO, and I lay in Creekstone Manor's dark and silent bedroom. My hands were clasped together across my stomach as I lay tucked under large fancy quilts, which lay heavy on my legs. I shifted, tapped a finger against my hand, and rolled onto my side.

How was any of this fair? I turned onto my side, arms crossed. James Cordington, off gallivanting in the forest alone to find *my* dragon. It was alive—or was it? Alive was not a very scientific term. What made a thing *alive*?

I tossed onto my other side and chewed at my lip. Miss Witherstine had been cross all through supper. Iris had seethed at me afterward, issuing another "warning" about Miss Witherstine. Still, it was nothing I couldn't handle…

There were two things, besides my dragon, that nagged at my heart.

The first was the danger Iris had warned me about. Miss Witherstine and her talent for gossiping someone into destruction was a real threat. If it were my reputation on the line, I could handle it…but Professor Booker took great steps to care for his reputation. It was why his workshop was in the back of his property—why he had chosen to live so far from any nosy neighbors. And while he was gone, he had no control over the situation. Lucky for him, *I did*. I had to keep the town from discovering the truth about the stones, the dragon, *everything*. This was the least I could do after how Professor Booker had taken care of me this past year.

But does the Professor really care for you?

I swallowed. The insidious whispers had been dormant for some hours. Each time it grew silent, a small hope formed in the center of my chest that it was the last time I'd hear its vile words.

I shook my head and turned onto my back. I stared up at the four posts on my bed and the sweeping, curtained canopy above me. I stared at the folds of fabric and bit my lip.

This led to the second thing. I didn't want to just hide the truth until Professor Booker came home. I wanted to understand the truth. The greatest scientific discovery was at my fingertips! If I figured out the secrets that my dragon held, I would become exactly what the Professor wanted me to be! His star pupil! Together, he and I would be the greatest inventors the world had ever seen.

I couldn't spend my time planning a stupid party and discovering scientific wonders at the same time, now could I?

Or could I?

I threw the thick quilts off. I quickly ran to the closet, scooped up my shoes, and slipped silently into a skirt and blouse. I tiptoed out of my room and eased the door shut.

I crept down the hall, past Miss Witherstine's closed bedroom door. I slipped down the stairs, my boots in my hand. I slipped into the kitchen and froze. There, on the counter, was a plate of unwrapped cookies.

My eyes darted around the darkened kitchen—the brass stove that gleamed from the moonlight that trickled through the window and the many shelves of ingredients to the right. Nobody else was down here. All was silent. Slowly, I eased into the room, around the counter, and toward the back door. I stopped again as I peeked out the window in the door. On the steps of the porch, two figures sat huddled together.

It was Iris. She sat, her arms wrapped tightly around the mayor's son, Albert Bamford Jr.

I scrunched my nose. Iris's head rested on Albert's shoulder. His arm was around her shoulders, his fingers gently rubbing her upper arm. I grinned, put one hand on the knob, and quickly opened the door.

The two shot apart immediately. Iris stood and whirled around to face me, her hands primly behind her, as Albert jumped for a nearby shrub.

"Lillian?" she whispered. "Why are you awake?"

"Why are *you*?" I snickered as I eased the door shut and jogged down the cobblestone steps. I glanced down at Albert, who was halfway hidden in the bushes, and then slowly turned to look at Lillian with a grin. "Does Miss Witherstine know about this?"

Iris glared. "About what?"

I clicked my tongue and crossed my arms. Iris mirrored my body language, though I could see her red cheeks in the moonlight. I snickered.

"Goodnight, Iris, I'll see you in the morning," I dipped my chin, twisted on my heel, and walked away. Behind me,

I heard a quiet whisper from the bushes.

"Do you think she saw me?"

I laughed and walked to the large oak tree. Every night, the front gates to Creekstone Manor were closed and locked, but lucky for me, I knew how to climb. I scrambled up to the bottom branch, its thick limb spreading just over the wall. I scooted forward and held onto the branch above, my legs dangling below me toward my freedom. I heard the crunch of gravel and looked into the gardens. Iris stood just under the tree, her hands on her hips.

"Lillian—what are you doing?" she whisper-yelled. "Get down from there or—"

"Or what?" I challenged. "You'll tell Miss Witherstine? How would you explain how you caught me?"

Iris shot a glance behind her and then glowered up at me.

"At least I'm not sneaking out of the property! That's dangerous. With the beasts about—"

"Surely *Albert* can handle them!" I grinned and let go of the branch. My stomach lurched as I fell, my braids trailing above my head. Then, I landed and rolled on the grass. I shook off the stray twigs and took off down the road, back on track to Professor Booker's house.

The sun had just begun to light the earth—the sky above a dull gray as I skipped past the gate and came to Professor Booker's house.

"James!" I called. He wasn't in the garden. I looked at the house and my eyes narrowed. All the lights were off. I skipped around the house and came to the field. At first glance, the windmill seemed normal. It was only when a breeze tickled my cheek that I realized the large cloth blades stood completely still. I sucked in a breath—Professor Booker's workshop! How could I have forgotten the destruction from yesterday?

I rushed across the field, dirt and mud flying from my shoes as I ran. I came to the door—crooked on its hinges. Slowly, I pushed it open.

"Oh—you're up early." James stood in the middle of the workshop. He held a wooden broom and Professor Booker's apron was wrapped around him, with his sleeves rolled up to his forearms. His hair was perfectly messy. I blinked and quickly looked away. The workshop was by no means how Professor Booker had left it…but it wasn't the disaster *I* had left it, either. James had certainly been hard at work.

All the broken wood and charred metal debris had been swept and categorized into three different piles. The first I assumed to be salvageable pieces. The second was trash. And the third…

"I wasn't sure if you could use those pieces," James explained and set back to sweeping. "Figured you could go through it yourself. Those vines really did a number on this place, didn't they?"

I took a step forward and smoothed out my skirt. "Did you find the dragon?"

"More like it found me. I came back into the workshop and, well…" James shook his head. He held up his forearm, tan, and—I blinked—covered in bandages. I looked up at James as he set back to sweeping. "Oh, don't worry. They're not deep. The little bugger just landed on me. I don't know if he even left the workshop…scared the dickens outta me when I came in here to clean up, but you were right. The dragon does not eat humans—so far. Hasn't seemed to set anything on fire, either. Oh, hey, how are your hands?"

"They're fine," I dismissed his inquiry. They'd scabbed over quickly. The cuts weren't deep. I stepped further into the workshop—the plants had all been cut and swept into the trash pile.

"Y'know, it's weird. The dragon, that is—well, *everything*. But really the dragon. Once you left…it sort of curled up under the table. It's sleeping now, so I assume. Hasn't moved." James nodded toward the dragon. It sat crouched under the table, eyes glowing a soft orange.

I grabbed my apron off the peg and slipped on a pair of leather gloves. "You can sweep later, James. We've experiments to run!"

"This is a bad idea."

I ignored James as I strapped a pair of Professor Booker's goggles around my head. I tightened the straps on either side to fit my head. My hair was tied up and into a bun. I tugged on the thick leather gloves. We stood in the barren field to the side of the windmill. I kept a watchful eye on Booker Lane and the road—ready for any carriages that would come and kidnap me. The dragon stood still, the only sign of its life in its fiery orange eyes.

"You're ready to take notes?" I asked. James and I had pulled half the broken workbench from the shop and set it against an old tree stump to form a makeshift desk.

He sat behind it on a turned over log, quill and parchment in hand.

"Equipped and ready!" he called as he waved them in the air. I nodded and turned back to the dragon.

"Good. Let the experiment begin!" I grinned. Professor Booker always said, "Anyone who was a true intellectual knew the basis of a good scientist wasn't really about how smart you were, or what you knew, but it was what kind of questions you asked."

I knew the reason the mechanical dragon was alive had to do with the rocks—and that I wasn't allowed anywhere near the rocks. Thus, all questions pertaining to the rocks themselves were ones I couldn't ask.

However, there were a few questions I *could* ask. First and foremost, did my dragon gain sentience?

The second thing any good scientist did was take that question and gather research. Again, something James and I couldn't do—but I would not be deterred. I was certain that this exact situation had never happened before in Kesterfield, let alone the world! Besides, Miss Witherstine would sooner or later notice my disappearance, so we were on a time crunch. Research would have to wait.

"Alright, let us mark our current hypothesis," I called as I walked toward the beast. The creature, around the size of a hound dog, sat curled in the grass, its tail flicking from side to side like a cat. I stopped about five feet from its head and stated, "That this creature is *not* alive."

James, from behind me, snorted.

I turned with a frown. "Do you disagree, *Mr. Cordington?*"

I watched as he waved the quill in the air and said, "No, no, not at all. It just occurs to me that yesterday you were yelling the exact *opposite* of our current hypothesis…"

"I was caught up in the excitement and made a hasty judgment—which is why we're here now," I huffed.

James, in turn, shrugged and dipped his quill in the ink. "I just think you're underestimating the amount of trouble we've gotten ourselves into is all. Carry on."

Professor Booker never would have been so quick to jump to a conclusion, and in the future, neither would I. I looked down at my dragon. It sat, staring at me with its orange eyes. I took a step closer. The creature tilted its head.

"The first series of tests pertain to this question—" I called back to James, who dutifully wrote down my words. "Does this creature display any sign of performing the following capabilities? Eating, excreting—James, it's *not* funny—breathing, growing, and responding to external stimuli. The first test—for the sake of putting your mind at ease, James—is eating!"

I pulled a red apple from the pocket of my leather apron. Carefully approaching the dragon, I held the apple out toward its jaw. The beast turned its head to the side.

"C'mon, uh…dragon," I clicked my tongue as if talking to a dog. "Take the apple—eat the apple—c'mon dragon—"

"It needs a name!" James called. I ignored him and kept my attention on what mattered.

I frowned as the dragon stared silently ahead. It didn't appear to be tempted by the fruit. I frowned and slowly took a bite of the apple—hastily wiping my chin as a bead of juice escaped. In hindsight, I hadn't built the thing to have a digestive tract. Obviously, it hadn't needed it. The original design was meant to help Professor Booker with whatever he needed. Perhaps the problem lay not with how the dragon was built but with the food. I looked down at the apple and frowned.

"Maybe it would be more interested in meat," James whispered, his breath tickling my ear. I flipped around, my eyes wide. He knelt close to me, our shoulders brushing.

"James!" I hissed. "You're supposed to be taking notes—"

"I am!" He held up the quill and paper. "Calm down—I am. I just wanted to get a better view of what I was taking notes on. Is that a crime?"

Suddenly, the previous day came to mind—his arms around my waist, my head on his shoulder—my cheeks flamed and I tore the goggles off. "James—I need *space* to be able to—"

And suddenly, I had all the space I needed. The dragon moved silently and swiftly. One moment, it had been sitting calmly behind me. The next, it had forced itself between me and James, its wings out and its mouth hissing dangerous black smoke. I fell back onto the ground, my eyes wide, as James scrambled back on all fours.

"Lillian—Lillian, it's—"

"Shh!" I waved James off as I inspected the creature. It stood still once more, and slowly, with a clicking of gears, the metallic wings folded back around its body.

"Does it seem bigger to you than it did yesterday?" James whisper-yelled from the front of the creature. I tapped my chin and slowly stood.

"Have you written any of this down?" I asked. I walked around the creature to the front and knelt by its head. James, behind me, huffed and began to furiously scribble on the parchment. I slowly reached out and touched my palm to the cool metal snout. The beast shifted but kept its orange eyes trained on James. I smoothed out my skirt and stood once again.

"James—did you see that?" I whispered. "It *obeyed* me—"

James looked up. "I hardly think—"

"Lillian! Where are you?"

We turned toward the house at the call. My stomach dropped.

"Lillian Booker!"

"Is that Iris?" James scrunched his nose. We both looked down at my dragon and then snapped our attention to each other once more.

You'll be discovered—she'll tell everyone how you disobeyed Professor Booker!

"Dragon—hide in the workshop!" I hissed as I threw off my gloves and shoved them into James's hands. "James—make sure it goes back inside!"

"Are you crazy?!" James hissed back. The dragon leaped up and bounded toward the workshop. James looked from my dragon to me, then tore after it, cursing under his breath. I snapped the goggles off my head and smoothed down my hair. I rounded the gravel pathway, turned the corner of Professor Booker's house, and screeched to a halt. Iris stood in front of me. Her hair was combed, and her hands were folded in front of her. I sucked in a breath and leaned against the wooden slats on the side of the house.

"Iris Witherstine, how good of you to stop by," I grinned. Iris didn't return my smile. Instead, I watched as her eyes narrowed. I swallowed and resisted the urge to glance behind me. "What are you doing here?"

"You know why I'm here." Iris crossed her arms. "It's nearly eight, and Miss Witherstine will be looking for you."

"Yes, she often seems to be looking for me," I inspected my fingernails. "I don't see how that explains *your* presence, now does it?"

Iris scoffed. "Oh, well then, please, stay here and let her wrath bore down on you and all that you love."

It was my turn to scoff. "Please, nothing can stop me from inventing, least of all Miss—"

"Oh, believe me, that wasn't *what* I was talking about. It's more about *who* I'm talking about," Iris bit back. My cheeks flamed as she nodded behind me. James rounded the corner, his grin tight and sleeves pulled down to cover the bandages. He softly waved.

"Good morning, Iris—"

"Good day," Iris curtsied, turned, and strode down the pathway. I swallowed, my mouth dry.

"What was *that* about?" James rested a hand on my shoulder. I shrugged it off and strode after Iris.

"I have to go!" I called behind me. "Take care of…*things*."

I refused to look back as I turned down the gravel pathway and began to trek back toward Creekstone Manor.

I'D SPENT THE ENTIRE MORNING party planning, and now, late into the evening, I sat, back painfully straight, at the coffee table in Miss Witherstine's parlor. A large pile of unfolded napkins sat to my left and a pitifully small pile of folded napkins to my right. Iris sat across the parlor, next to the cook. They chatted quietly as they polished the forks. Already, they'd finished with all the teaspoons, which sat shining in a small basket.

"Now, up, up, a little to the left—" Miss Witherstine's words rang out in the parlor. She faced the two servants who stood on either side of the large fireplace. They balanced precariously on wooden ladders, a long banner with the words *"Happy Birthday"* scrawled across.

I huffed and turned back to the cloth napkins. They scratched at my hands, the feeling radiating from my tender scabs to just under my fingernails.

We need to escape.

I shifted and tried to ignore that thought. After all, how could one think of parties and planning and *stupid* social gatherings when the next technological breakthrough was at your fingertips? I yearned for the night to be over—experimenting could be done in the windmill with torches and lights. I just had to wait for Miss Witherstine and Iris to retire for the night...

They'll never accept us.

I ignored the whisper in my head and continued to ponder what had happened that morning. Our findings were inconclusive. I hadn't had enough time to properly observe everything that *needed* observing. Why had it jumped between us? Was it obeying a command?

We don't belong here.

I shifted and looked back toward the large windows. The light outside had fallen past the trees and hills, making the landscape a deep brownish black and the sky a deepening gray. The lights in the town had begun to flicker on... I narrowed my eyes. Only two lights seemed to be without a flicker—they were an even space apart and a deeper orange...

My stomach dropped as I saw past my reflection in the window and recognized the face of my dragon.

I stood and the napkins tumbled from my lap. I stumbled back, my heart hammering inside my chest. I seized the long satin curtains and tugged—they didn't budge. I tugged again.

"Lillian, darling," Miss Witherstine called from across the parlor. "Is everything alright?"

I spun around, the curtain caught in my hands. My eyes snapped to Iris and the cook, both of whom had stopped polishing and now stared at me. I swallowed.

"Yes!" I looked to Miss Witherstine. "Oh, yes, yes, I'm fine. I just—we don't want strangers looking in on us to spoil the surprise for Professor Booker, now do we?"

Miss Witherstine and Iris shared a glance.

"The curtains are just decor, love," Miss Witherstine said. I let the curtain fall from my hands.

"Oh." I laughed—too tight and just a pitch too loud for it to be natural. I quickly scooped up the napkins and set them on the table. I looked at the dragon from the corner of my eye. It watched me, unblinking, metal teeth pulled back into a tight grin—almost like the one I had just worn. I looked back down at the napkins and began to fold.

I knew James—he wouldn't abandon his watch of the creature on purpose, would he? Which could only mean one thing.

Whatever the rock had or *hadn't* done, there was no denying it. My dragon had a will of its own and had escaped the workshop. Interesting that it had chosen to follow me. Perhaps it had bonded to me. Or respected me as its creator, wishing to do as I commanded. That would explain what had happened that morning.

My hands itched, and I pressed my lips firmly together. Free will—a tricky subject. I swallowed and set the napkin to the right, then slowly glanced over to the window.

For the second time that night, my stomach dropped. My dragon was gone.

I snapped my head back to the table. Quietly, methodically, I smoothed out my skirt and stood.

"Whatever is the problem, Lillian?" Miss Witherstine asked in a calm and soothing voice. I could only imagine what terrors lay underneath such a mask.

"I…" I hesitated and glanced out the window. "I need the restroom. Excuse me."

I forced myself to walk slowly. To keep my shoulders down and relaxed, my face set into a comfortable smile. The moment I had eased the parlor door shut, I shot off like a mouse through the hallways, into the kitchen and out the back door.

"Psst! Here…dragon—come here!" I frowned. James was right. We should have named it. I shook my head and set down the garden path. My boots crunched the gravel as I traveled down the winding pathways of the garden. The moon poked up from behind the house but didn't give much light to guide my way. I stumbled through a planter and came to the tree. I walked around the large oak and stopped.

The wall was tall and magnificent and utterly perfect… well…it *had been* perfect. Now, long and jagged claw marks marred the gray surface of the stone wall. I swallowed and took a step forward. My hand brushed the exposed stone, the claw marks an inch or so deep.

I followed them up until I couldn't reach them. The marks led to the very top of the wall and then disappeared from view.

I rolled up my sleeves and clambered up the tree. I shifted and climbed to the top of the wall. I shimmied over to the marks. My eyes narrowed as I tried to make them out in the moonlight.

"Huh." I scrunched my nose. There, at the top along the edge, it was as though the dragon had gripped the stone and… and then nothing. The marks stopped and didn't continue down the other side of the wall.

"Lillian!" I looked down toward the back road. James stood on the dirt path, his hands cupped around his mouth. "Lillian, the dragon's gone and—"

"I know!" I hissed back. "It was outside the parlor just a second ago!"

I heard a crunch on the gravel and spun toward the garden. Iris stood just a few feet away, her arms crossed and eyebrows raised.

"I can understand some sneaking off, but right in front of Miss Witherstine? Do you have a death wish?"

I looked from her back to James, eyes wide.

"James Cordington, *I assume*, is on the other side of that wall," Iris spoke as she picked her way off the path. She raised her skirt with a delicate hand and stood just under the tree. She looked up, and for a moment, I wondered if she genuinely cared for me and my reputation. Then her eyes narrowed and she said, "I swear to you, Lillian. James Cordington is a respectable boy, and you're—"

"I'm *what?*" I snapped, my voice pitched higher.

Disgraceful. Shameful. Not worthy.

I shook my head. "I am *not* sneaking off to see James Cordington!"

Iris raised a slender eyebrow.

"Is that Iris?" James whisper-yelled from the path. I suppressed a glare. He started to clamber toward us up the grassy hill. "Hey—tell her to get back inside!"

"James!" I hissed. We needed a distraction—something to distract Iris from my constant sneaking. Iris shook her head.

"Lillian, please. Just get down and come back inside! Miss Witherstine will be furious!"

I slapped both my hands over my ears, straddling the wall. What a terrible situation! This is why I stayed in the workshop!

"Iris! Hey—Iris!" James called from the bottom of the wall. Iris scowled from the other side.

"Go *away*, Mr. Cordington!" Iris snapped. "Lillian is not—"

"Iris, you have to get inside!" James continued. "We're in a dangerous situation here—"

Iris scoffed. "At least one of you agrees with me. Besides, I think—"

Iris snapped her mouth shut and suddenly pressed her back to the tree. My hands itched, and I brought them away from my ears. Above me, I heard the distinct sound of chittering gears. The wind kicked up around me, my skirt flapping in the gust. I looked up into the sky and my mouth dropped.

Above us, the dragon beat its wings, its body three times the size it had been just that morning.

"Jiminy cricket—how did it get so big?!" James shrieked from below me. Its wings flapped, strong and powerful. Gears and metal creaked as my dragon craned its neck to stare at me, its reddish orange eyes glowing like stars in the night.

"Lillian—" Iris shrieked. "*What is that?*"

The dragon's wings beat, the gears churning and grinding together. I grabbed onto a nearby branch and, carefully, stood atop the wall.

"What are you doing!?" James cried.

At the same time, Iris shrieked, "Are you insane!? *Get down!*"

I grit my teeth, and with my arms balanced out beside me, surged forward.

"You!" I called up to the dragon. Its face was focused on... something in the distance. "I created you—you must obey!"

"You did *what?*" Iris cried.

I was subtly aware of James slapping his hand against his forehead.

"Lillian—get down!" James yelled. "*It's going to eat you!*"

"Eat her?" Iris shrieked. Immediately, the two began screaming opposite directions at me, their words crashing together and mixing with the mechanical beat and whir of the wings above us. I squeezed my hands together, teeth clenched. My mind raced as I tried to think of something—anything to distract Iris. To get her away from me and James.

The dragon soared into the night air and toward the town. James hissed and walked backward, neck craned back as he tried to keep his eyes on the beast. Iris rushed to the wall and began to jump, grabbing for my shoes.

"Get down—get down—get down!" she shrieked.

You aren't safe. They'll discover your lies.

I stayed still, listening to the venomous whisper in my brain.

Don't you wish this perfect little town with its perfect little people would leave us alone?

I didn't need to answer the question. Anxiety clenched my stomach, and I feared that I'd just commanded the beast to do something I'd come to regret. I had to see why it had headed to town.

I jumped down and landed with a thud next to Iris. Then, I snatched her hand and took off. Iris stumbled behind me.

"Where are we going? We have to get—"

I spun around and slapped both my hands over her mouth.

"Listen!" I hissed. Her eyes widened. Our shoulders rose and fell as we caught our breath. I continued. "There are two irrefutable facts. The first, that dragon you just saw is headed for the town. The second, Miss Witherstine would be inconsolable were she to know about this. We've no time to console her *and* stop the beast from whatever it's about to do. We have to protect the town!"

Iris smacked my hands away. She took a second to suck in a deep breath through her nostrils.

"Fine," she stuck out her hand. "But you have to promise to

tell Albert about this. He needs to know."

I sucked in a breath as I thought of my dragon being hunted by the Defense Team. I glanced to the sky, toward the town, then back at Iris.

"Fine," I lied. "I'll tell him."

"Okay," she whispered, and her shoulders fell in relief. She reached out, grabbed my hand, and gave it a squeeze. "What do we do?"

Relief like a fresh spring washed over me. I tightened my grasp, and together, we rushed through the gardens and out the large wrought iron gate that had yet to be locked for the night.

"Lillian—" James faltered as he saw Iris.

"The beast—the town—it's flying toward the town!" I huffed between breaths. "Let's go!"

Together, the three of us hit the cobblestone road. Our footsteps echoed as we ran.

FIND THE DRAGON. The lights around the town flickered as the three of us tore through the streets. Find the dragon. I sucked in a breath, the cool air hitting my lungs and scratching my throat as I turned in a circle, staring at the sky above me.

"This afternoon—" James huffed next to me. "As I cleaned—I can't believe we didn't realize this sooner—"

"Spit it out!" I cried. Clouds had rolled over the pale moon, the stars blinking and twinkling high above.

"It was bigger—not by much, but it was definitely bigger this morning," James ran a hand through his hair. "Lilly—what do we—"

"There!" Iris screamed. She pointed toward the church steeple. "It's by the church!"

The three of us were off once more. My heart hammered in my chest, and a sinking, sickly feeling invaded my stomach and twisted in my intestines. We traveled over perfect cobblestone streets and past perfectly constructed houses with perfect little gardens and decorations.

Perfect—why was it all so *perfect?*

I heard a crash, followed quickly by the clatter of metal and shattering wood. James and I shared a glance and continued to run.

Iris followed, just steps behind us. We rounded the curved corner of Basker Avenue and stopped in front of the church. I scanned the skies, staring up at the steeple. The clouds parted, and moonlight shone on the brass speaker at the top of the church.

"Lillian—" James grabbed my shoulder. I turned toward him and froze.

A small fire blazed from a stand in the center of the market. The flames leaped up from the splintered and charred wood. The smoke billowed into the sky in a twirling dance. The stalls around the market looked as though they'd been crushed, like a bug underneath a boot.

Beside me, James leaped into action toward the well. Iris and I stood next to each other. Above us, a dark shape soared off toward the forest and then vanished into the clouds. We watched as James doused the flames. He coughed, ran back to the well and grabbed another bucket. I tugged on my braids.

Why? Why would my dragon do this?

"It's—gone!" James breathed out in a hurried whisper as he approached with the empty bucket in his hand. "The fire's out but…the market it's…"

"First Professor Booker's workshop." I closed my eyes. "Now the market…"

Professor Booker is going to be furious with you.

The time for scientific discovery was over. My dragon had officially gotten out of hand. I swallowed thickly as I looked at the market, charred and destroyed. I thought of

Mr. Bennett. What would he do? How would he sell his goods? I felt the pressure begin to build behind my eyes, and I closed them.

If the town discovered the dragon, I would disgrace Professor Booker. *His* inventions helped the town. I would not let his reputation be marred.

Iris pulled at her skirt, her face pale.

"Alright—James," I turned to him. "The dragon went to the forest. We need to follow it—"

James motioned to the market. "Follow it? Lillian—it destroyed everything!"

"And it'll destroy *more* if we don't stop it." I clenched my hands into fists. "Professor Booker told you to help me, so *help me*."

James sucked in a breath, eyes wide. He looked hurt, as though I'd slapped him across the cheek. "Okay," he whispered, "I'll help. Whatever you need, Lilly."

Now you've done it. He'll never forgive you for this.

Fear like I'd never known gripped me and my heart stuck in my throat. I turned roughly away.

"We're going into the forest and we're finding my dragon. I think if I can speak to it, I can convince it to stop. Under no circumstances are we going to tell anybody what's happening. Am I understood?" I barked.

Iris's eyebrows scrunched together. "But you said we'd get Albert—"

"We've no time for your boyfriend, Iris!" I snapped. "The dragon is getting away—let's go!"

I took off down the lane, Iris and James following close behind. Together, we ran into the forest.

THE THREE OF US RAN through the forest. The leaves and twigs tore at our clothes and exposed cheeks as we followed the dark shape in the sky.

Iris screamed as her foot caught on a branch, and she fell. I slid to a stop.

"I'll keep going!" James shouted as he launched over a bush and vanished past the trees. "Make sure she's okay!"

I hesitated—my heart beat rapidly. I took a step toward the path James had taken and then, with a grunt, turned around and walked back toward Iris.

"Iris," I knelt by her side and helped her sit up. Dirt dusted her chin. A bead of blood slid from her knee and down her leg. She sniffed and wiped hurriedly at her face. I sat back and gave her some space. "Are you...alright?"

"No," Iris hissed. "*You* said we were protecting the town!"

My stomach clenched.

"We are!" I said. "If we find my dragon, we—"

"No, you're not stopping anything. You're lying!" she bit back. Tears brimmed in her eyes. "We need to call Albert and Miss Witherstine—"

"Why?" I threw my hands in the air. "It's not hurting anyone! If we get it back into the workshop, I can—"

"What? Dismantle it? Use one of your inventions to take care of it?" Iris sneered. I swallowed thickly.

"Yes. *I would.* If it came to it, I'd…I'd destroy it."

Iris's mouth dropped open, aghast. "You don't see it… you're so blind."

"See what?" I snapped. Iris scooted forward on her knees.

"You're so blinded by your desperation that you don't even see the danger it's put you in—*it's put all of us in!*"

I scoffed. "Desperation? What could *I* possibly be *desperate* for?"

The wind picked up around us. Dust swirled in the air. A giant shadow fell over us, and I looked up at the sky. The dragon—my dragon—hovered in the sky above the treetops. I peered past the leaves and branches above me, trying to catch a proper look at the beast. I gasped as I realized that my dragon was now the size of a small house. I scooted back as the metal on its belly began to glow orange. Iris screamed, but all I could do was focus on the creature. Bushes and twigs snapped as James came tumbling back through the brush.

"Get down!" James grabbed both of our hands and brought us under the shade of a tree. We crouched low as the dragon hovered. Its head moved as though it were scanning the trees below, and then it took off into the night sky and vanished from sight.

"We…that thing could *kill* someone." Iris sucked in a breath. "It already destroyed the market! We have to—to tell—"

"Shut up!" I hissed.

Iris continued to cry. "Lillian, you—"

I slapped my hands over her mouth. Her back slammed into the tree.

"Lillian!" James yelped. Iris sucked in a breath through her nose, her eyes wide, tears collecting in the corners.

I pressed on. "Iris, you have to promise me you won't tell!"

I gagged as I felt her tongue slip between my fingers. I retracted my hands and landed on my rump as she scrambled to sit up.

"I *have* to tell—Miss Witherstine! If she finds out I knew and—"

"*I'll tell her about you and Albert!*" The threat left my lips before I'd even had time to think. I saw her eyes flash with pain. Her lips pressed together, thin and tight. I swallowed, my heart burning.

"You wouldn't," she finally whispered. I sucked in a breath.

"Oh, Miss Witherstine, you must be so proud of Iris," I whispered. Panic had an icy grip on my heart. I clenched my fists and barreled on, unthinking. "How long has she been courting the mayor's son? Oh, you didn't know? My, that's embarrassing—"

"Enough," Iris whispered, "…I won't tell."

And in that silence, we both stood. I dusted off my skirt, smoothing the hair out of my face with shaking, itching hands. Iris turned away. I watched as she swiped hastily at her cheeks. My stomach lurched.

You had to do this.

"But I refuse to further cooperate in such a thing," she whispered. She nodded to James, picked up her skirt, and marched back toward the town.

I SMOOTHED MY HAIR BACK, my eyes shut. How did things go so wrong so fast?

"Come along," I muttered as I turned back toward the forest. "Let's go."

"So, I'm supposed to ignore what just happened?" James snapped. I stopped and my shoulders dropped. James continued, "Just like always, then."

"What? *What* is there to talk about?" I whirled around. "Iris was going to betray us—she'd tell Miss Witherstine *everything* and then—"

"And then get us some help that we *probably* need," he pointed out. "She's trying to be your friend."

"I never asked for her to be my friend!" I hissed. "And I don't remember ever asking *you*, either. What are you still doing here, James?"

James shut his mouth, eyes wide. I took a ragged breath and stalked toward him.

"Did Professor Booker *really* ask you to help? Or are you sticking around, waiting to be his '*favorite apprentice*' again?"

"No—*Lillian*—" James clenched his jaw. He turned away from me and let out a deep and pained groan. "You're *so* paranoid!"

"And you're intrusive!" I accused. "Always demanding to know what I'm thinking, what I'm feeling—why? Why does it matter to you?"

James shut his eyes. I watched as his shoulders fell, and he stared ahead with dull honey-brown eyes. His cheeks had taken a red hue, and his fists were clenched at his side.

I turned away and whispered, "Go home, James."

I walked forward, past the bushes, and ignored the way my stomach suddenly ached. I didn't have time for this. I had a dragon to find.

I leaned against a tree and stared with tired eyes at Professor Booker's windmill.

The sunrise cast pastel pink and purple streaks on the gray sky. Iris was back home, probably telling Miss Witherstine everything…James had finally found sense, done what was best for himself, and left. The sun had just begun to rise over the trees.

I ran a hand over my eyes. I felt fatigued like I hadn't felt since I'd come to the perfect little town of Kesterfield. It wore down my bones till they felt brittle. My eyes were heavy and dark. My hair tangled with twigs and leaves. I wasn't sure how…but in the past year, I'd managed to forget what this fatigue had felt like…but now I remembered. It hung on me like a heavy weight.

Slowly, I pushed myself off the tree and began to make

my way through the desolate field surrounding Professor Booker's home.

A bell tolled from town. I stopped. My feet sunk into the dusty ground. I blinked. Was it Sunday already? No, no, it wasn't. I still had a day or so. I continued walking. The bell sounded off again, followed by an echoing crackle as the speaker inside the church steeple turned on.

"Town emergency—town emergency—seek shelter at the church immediately," Albert Bamford Jr.'s voice echoed through the town and over the sweeping hills. "A beast has been sighted—come take shelter at the church immediately."

The words echoed in my ears, sending a chill down my spine. My stomach dropped. I picked up my skirt and rushed toward Professor Booker's house.

I KEPT MY SHOULDERS STRAIGHT, my back pressed against the hard wooden bench of the church pew. People milled around me, their voices low as they gossiped with one another. A pit steadily grew in my stomach.

I stared up at the Mother Mary's cold, hard eyes and couldn't help but see a resemblance to another highly revered woman I knew. What would Mother Mary say to me, I wondered, if she knew all I'd done and said in the past week?

Harlot.

I held in a scoff and looked away.

"Lillian—psst!"

I glanced over my shoulder. Mrs. Cordington sat just behind me, her blonde hair hidden in a bonnet, her eyes a sweet brown like her son's. They sent a pang of guilt through my heart, and I looked at her hands, which were clasped tightly together in her lap.

"Have you seen James?"

I shrugged and shook my head. Mrs. Cordington pursed her lips and sat back in the pew.

A man cleared his throat, and I turned back around to face the front.

The mayor, instead of the preacher, stood at the front of the church behind the podium. He wore his hair combed back, his bowler hat tucked under his thick arm, his hair just starting to speckle with gray. His eyes darted around the room, beady and small, as he spoke in quiet, hushed tones to the board members next to him. I couldn't read his lips past his large brown mustache, cleaned and oiled to perfection, unlike the wild and untamed beard of the Professor.

The market had been found, *obviously*. Nothing I could have done would have stopped that from happening. I fiddled with my skirt. Iris sat stiff next to me. Miss Witherstine sat next to Iris, deep in a hushed conversation with another woman behind us.

The mayor cleared his throat and stepped up to the podium. He shushed the crowd with his hands, then gripped either side of the podium. "N-now, now, let's calm down. I-I have a statement that needs to be made."

Miss Witherstine turned and faced forward. I kept my shoulders still. It wasn't my fault the market was destroyed. I had done everything I could! Yet, I couldn't help the nagging feeling of dread in my chest.

"Now, I-I don't think it'll come as a shock to any of you when I tell you that our, uh, our beloved market where we sell many fine goods and crops from our lovely farmers—has uh, has been destroyed by…something." He looked into the crowd, subtly grabbed a white cloth from his breast pocket, and wiped his brow. "Our, uh, *my* son, Albert Jr., hasn't found anything, uh, conclusive as of yet. B-but we suspect it was not one of the beasts from the quarry. Rest assured, we are doing everything uh, everything in our power to find out where this beast is. Now—we're going to ask you to come forward if you uh, if you have any information regarding what's taken place here, please, uh…don't be shy."

Iris stiffened next to me. In the front row, I saw Albert Jr. with his friends in the Defense Team. I shut my eyes and took a slow breath in through half-parted lips.

"Yes—Miss Witherstine?"

My eyes flashed open. Miss Witherstine had stood up, her hands crossed gently in front of her. Iris stared down at the floor, her eyes dark.

"Well, I must say, *I* didn't see anything," she placed a hand on Iris's shoulder and squeezed. I felt the room begin to spin. I was going to puke. Miss Witherstine continued, "But I know that at some point in the evening, my sweet, little darling Iris and…Lillian Booker went out for a stroll together around town—as good, amiable, and educated young ladies should. Once Iris returned, she went straight to bed and had a pale look about her. I'm sure *they* saw something…Iris, dear?"

She looked down at Iris, who looked between me and the back of Albert's head. Slowly, Iris took a deep breath. She smoothed out her skirt and kept her eyes glued to the pew in front of her.

"I-I—" Her lips quivered.

"Speak up," Miss Witherstine hissed. Iris straightened.

"I saw a great beast!" I stood, my voice carrying through the church. I refused to look at Mother Mary's eyes as I continued. "I…it probably smelled meat or some other sort of produce left behind from the day's wares. *It* destroyed the market…"

I wasn't lying, I told myself. I *had* seen a beast.

Iris stared at me, face pale. I swallowed and turned back toward the mayor.

"A beast?" he asked, disdain dripping from his tongue. He raised his eyebrows, and a few chuckles echoed around the church. "Impossible. My son would have been able to track it."

"Sit down," Miss Witherstine hissed between clenched teeth. "This isn't proper—"

"*I*..." My voice wavered. I clenched my fist over my heart. "I do not think it will return, so—"

"It's true! There was a great beast—huge!"

I flipped around. Standing on the far wall was an old man who owned the plot of land across from Professor Booker's. His voice shook as he stood—his hair was icy white and his face was a deep, sunburned red. He locked eyes with me and nodded slowly.

"My cows—herd of cows," he continued. "The beast swooped down from the sky and ate *three* of my cows!"

My hands dropped to my side and I rubbed my itchy palms over my skirt. I...I wasn't lying. But was he?

"Wait—he's right, I saw it too! The beast soared through the sky just last night!" Mr. Bennett stood. Slowly, the little church became crowded with chatter. Each person rose to their feet and told the hideous tale of the beast. It had gotten in their trash bins, their livestock—stolen someone's new carriage. The noise of everyone speaking at once clawed into my ears and beat against my brain. It had made a mess of every perfect thing in Kesterfield.

My head spun.

You have to protect yourself.

The voice in my head rose above the thundering shouts around me. My gut dropped.

You'll never be safe in this town—with these perfect people and their perfect standard.

I looked back toward the farmer and sucked in a breath. There was no hiding anymore. Something drastic had to be done. My dragon was out of control.

"Enough—al-alright," the mayor raised his hands again. He waved downwards as he continued, "Let's calm down. Al-alright, now…right. The uh, the safety of the town is, of course, our top priority. Let's uh…well, we'll talk to everyone who saw the beast, line them up, and uh, gather as much information as we—"

"Well, Mayor Bamford, if I may be so blunt…" Miss Witherstine's shrill voice carried. "I think what needs to be done is obvious." I felt my heart drum against my chest.

The mayor paused. "O-oh?"

Another beat, deep and hard, against my ribs. Miss Witherstine smiled. "We need to hunt and kill the creature. For the safety of the town and our livelihoods. Send out the town's Defense Team!"

The hair on the back of my neck rose—my palms suddenly clammy. The mayor paused to swallow. He again swiped a cloth over his shiny forehead.

"N-now, I'm uh, I'm not sure we should send our young men out, unprepared for whatever violence—"

"It's not violence." Miss Witherstine looked aghast. "It's called *protection*. We must do this for our children! If the beast ate a cow, surely one of our young ones is next! We've no time!"

I shook my head numbly. It wouldn't do that! My dragon couldn't do that.

"She's right—we have children to protect!" A woman from across the room stood, a baby held tight to her chest.

"Mouths to feed—" A farmer stood.

Another man stood. "How are we supposed to track the beast? We've no equipment for such a task, and if it flies—"

"We need Professor Booker," the farmer snapped. "Miss Witherstine, surely you can—"

"The Professor is on his birthday trip," Miss Witherstine bristled. "Surely, this is something we, as *adults*, can handle ourselves."

"I can track it!" The shout had left my mouth before I'd even known I was going to say anything. I could feel every eye turn to me as the room stilled. Miss Witherstine clicked her tongue. I rapidly blinked my eyes, steadied my breath, and continued, "Professor Booker has many inventions and…as his *niece*, I've learned how to use them. I…can use one of his machines to track down the beast."

"Brilliant!" The mayor grinned for the first time that meeting. "That's—yes, truly magnificent. Please—hurry and collect his inventions. We'll assemble the Defense Team here, waiting for you."

I dared not look at Miss Witherstine, whose eyes I could feel digging into my flesh. I exited the pew. Behind me, the mayor continued to prattle on with instructions. Iris sat, staring uncertainly after me as I went.

I swung open the large wooden door and slipped outside into the morning sun.

THE WORKSHOP DOOR SLAMMED SHUT behind me. My heels clicked against the cobblestone as I rushed across the debris and mutilated metal around me.

There was a single, complicated question I had to ask myself. How do you accomplish an impossible task (keep my dragon away from the town forever) in a short amount of time (preferably an hour or so) while saving your dignity (not letting the people around you realize the danger you caused) and the reputation of those who have cared for you?

The short answer? Lie like your life depends on it.

Unlike the people of Kesterfield, I knew that the dragon wasn't a real beast but was a machine. Granted, it had what *appeared* to be sentience, but it was a machine nonetheless. And there was only one thing that made this machine tick.

That stupid red rock.

I flung open drawers in the Professor's workshop, scrambling the tools and equipment inside as I searched for an item I had sworn I would never touch unless under the Professor's supervision—Professor Booker's hand cannon.

I wasn't supposed to experiment on the rocks…and technically, I wasn't experimenting on them.

I was going to destroy it—destroy it before anyone knew how the beast came about or why it was set on destroying the town.

The door squeaked on its hinges as it opened.

"Not *now*, James! I'm busy—" I spun around and stopped. My eyes widened, and slowly, I leaned back, shutting the drawer with my hip.

"Miss Witherstine," I acknowledged her presence with a sneer. She stood in the doorway, her hair wispy and falling from the perfect bun it was usually restrained in. Quickly, I set back to searching.

"What happened in here?" her voice warbled as she took in the plants piled in the corner. The deep cracks in the wood and stone floor. The metal shavings that littered the ground.

"*Science*," I answered curtly. "Now, I've got a very important task, and I—"

"Will be coming straight home," Miss Witherstine announced.

My nostrils flared. "I'm *busy*, Miss Witherstine."

Miss Witherstine stalked forward until she stood in front of me. "I'll not have a young lady such as yourself gallivanting *alone* through the woods—Why, if the beast came and gobbled you up, what would I tell—"

I sidestepped around her.

"Someone needs to save the town," I hissed. "Unlike *some* adults in charge of young wards, Professor Booker cares more about *morals* than how others perceive him!"

"Ha!" Miss Witherstine barked. "Perception. *Morals.* You've no idea who your Professor truly is. What he's done in his life. You stand here and speak to *me* about his *morals*…"

My stomach clenched.

"And who do you say he is?" I scoffed. I circled around her, teeth bared. "You, with your—your financial manipulation!"

"Financial manipulation?" her voice squeaked. Her eyes turned to slits. "I *support* him—"

"So long as he does what you ask! So long as he goes where you send! So long as he tells you everything he's doing!" I sucked in a breath. My cheeks felt warm, my head dizzy. "How do you know him when he must be on his best behavior in front of you? How do you know anyone when you demand—demand *perfection*?"

"Oh, and I suppose you know people." She clicked her tongue. "Hiding away in the attic, building useless scraps in a pathetic imitation of Johnathon. With your careless attitude and cheeky tongue."

I clenched my jaw tight. I could almost imagine steam building inside my chest, tangling with my heart and mind.

"The people of Kesterfield have no idea that they've harbored the true beast in Creekstone Manor this whole time!" I spit.

Miss Witherstine lowered her clenched fists to her side. She held her shoulders back and her chin high as she walked decidedly toward me once more. Quickly, I backed up.

"Oh, they have no idea who I am?" Her tone turned sweet, like coffee mixed with too much sugar. "Wait until they hear that their darling Professor harbors the daughter of a harlot!"

I backed into the stone wall. My head spun. She knew? She knew this whole time. Miss Witherstine stopped just inches from me. I glared up at her. She clicked her tongue and slowly shook her head.

"I despised your mother, you know...she was a temptress at

heart, even before she threw herself at the other men," Miss Witherstine whispered as she stared down at me. "But Johnathon…he was smitten."

"You *know?*" I asked, my voice cracking. "You know that *I'm his…*"

Miss Witherstine nodded. "Johnathon made a mistake… His actions could be forgotten—if you were not here, putting him and everything he's worked for at risk! I tried to convince you to be a lady—an upstanding citizen. If the truth were to be revealed, we could cover it. Unfortunately, you are just like your mother. Running around, fooling with a young man's heart…I wonder what James Cordington would say if he were to find out, hmm?"

My heart froze.

Weak. Pathetic. Useless.

"You don't deserve Johnathon," Miss Witherstine hissed.

I swallowed the lump in my throat. The edges of my eyes pricked with unshed tears. Slowly, with as even a tone I could muster, I whispered, "And you do?"

"*Yes.*" She hissed between her perfect white teeth. "I am a refined, dignified woman. People of Kesterfield *respect* me. Now, you are coming back to Creekstone Manor, and you are going to stay there until Johnathon returns. Are we clear?"

I clenched my fists and stared up at her. The shame I had grown comfortable in wrapped its heavy arms around my stomach. It clung to my back like a thick layer of mud and grime. I lowered my gaze. "*Perfectly.*"

"Good." Miss Witherstine looked down at my hands. She pursed her lips, snatched up my wrist, and walked briskly out the door, tugging me behind her. "Let's *go.*"

THE GUTTER HAD BEEN WHERE I had first heard the insidious whisper inside my head. I'd been told to sit outside the shack we called home. It was a small thing with four cracked wooden walls, a tin roof, and a single glass window caked in dirt. I was always told to sit outside the shack while my mother stayed inside, entertaining.

As usual, a man approached from the back alley, his hat pulled low, his collar yanked up. I watched with narrowed eyes as the man shuffled past the garbage bins and stepped up to the doorway. He paused, glanced toward me, and hesitated.

"Hello, young lady," he nodded. I sat stiff, my legs pulled up to my chest. The men shouldn't speak to me—Mother had made that clear. Whenever one of them did, I'd get a pit the size of a rock inside my stomach. But this man was different from the rest. He had shocking white hair that stuck out from the edges of his hat like pieces of straw, and his eyes…almost seemed to shine. The man pressed his lips together, tipped his hat to me, and then knocked three times on the wooden door. It squeaked open, and he disappeared inside.

I had prepared to sit out there in the cold, damp weather for another hour when voices came from the shack.

"Impossible—" the man's voice carried from inside the shack. I straightened and looked behind me, eyes narrowed. "I see the way you live—if you think you can blackmail me—"

"I didn't live this way twelve years ago, Johnathon!" My mother's voice. "Need I remind you, we were engaged!"

"An engagement *you* broke off," the man, Johnathon, continued to shout. "I did not travel out here—leave my work and my apprentice just to come here and listen to you sully my name, my reputation!"

I crouched low and pressed my ear against the grimy glass window.

"Then why did you come?" my mother's voice dropped low. The man sighed.

"I shouldn't have," the man muttered. "A part of me hoped… but no, I can see you're still…the same. We're through."

"Test her!" my mother barked. "She's yours, Johnathon. I can see it in her eyes. She's smart—smarter than I ever could be. Just last week, she fixed all the locks in here with garbage she'd stolen from our neighbor's bins! Do whatever you need to prove it, but I know…you are her father."

There was silence in the shack. I scurried along the ground and pressed an ear to the cracked walls of my home.

"Why now?" the man, Johnathon, whispered. I held my breath as I listened.

"She's…become a distraction to my work. I can't have her stealing my clients, Johnathon. It's not…she's not safe and… you're a good man, Johnathon Booker…I hoped or thought…"

Silence permeated the shack.

"I understand," Johnathon finally whispered.

And then I heard it. A faint, stab-you-through-the-heart sort of thought.

She wants you gone because she doesn't love you. Nobody does.

I'd accepted it right then and there. No other plausible conclusion could have been drawn from what I'd heard. My mother wanted me gone. The man was being blackmailed into taking me. I had no choice, and nobody loved me.

I heard that voice again as Miss Witherstine marched through Professor Booker's garden.

Nobody loves you.

I grit my teeth. I felt my cheeks flame. We continued past the gate and into her carriage. The door shut, and we began to rumble down the road.

This was all Miss Witherstine's fault! With her perfect gardens and her perfect hair and need for everything around her to be perfect! I clenched my fist and glared straight ahead at the woman, not bothering to hide my contempt.

She shifted yet said nothing. Nothing! How could she live with herself?

You're not safe with her. Nobody is safe with her.

My hands itched. I clicked my tongue, glared down at them, and stopped. There—in my hands, just inside the scabs along my palms…was that… I lifted my hands to my eyes. My heart stopped.

Red flecks of dust glowed and swirled just inside my veins.

I hadn't thought to clean the cuts I'd gotten when the workshop had gone haywire—nor had I thought that *I* would need to be part of the experimentation and science we had conducted previously. What were the effects of magic stones *in* human flesh?

"Miss Witherstine—" I set my hands palms-down in my lap. "With Professor Booker gone, the town is in incredible danger. I'm the only one who can—"

"Lillian, we are *women*." Miss Witherstine rolled her eyes. "We don't save the town, and we don't invent things. That's what the *men* are for. Now, I can make subtle excuses for your ungraceful behaviors because of the inferiority of your birth, but I cannot excuse you from tarnishing Professor Booker's name."

"You are in danger!" I leaned forward, stressing each word. She paused, her eyes wide and lips parted. I continued. "There's more to this situation than you could possibly know, so get over yourself and take me back to the workshop before—"

The carriage lurched to a stop. I fell forward and landed atop Miss Witherstine's skirt. She kicked me as she scrambled up.

"Driver! What's going on? Driver!" she shrieked as she poked a head out of the carriage window. I huffed my hair out of my face and scrambled for the carriage door.

I slipped out the door, took three quick steps away, and then stopped.

Flames blazed from inside Creekstone's stone wall. Thick black smoke rolled into the sky. The speaker from town crackled, the sound echoing through Kesterfield.

"Fire—Creekstone Manor—there's a fire at Creekstone Manor!"

Behind me, a crowd of people had started to gather.

"Iris!" Miss Witherstine shrieked as she landed on the gravel next to me. "Iris, where are you? Iris!"

"Miss Witherstine—" I bit down on my tongue as she ran toward her home. The driver leaped off the carriage and grabbed her shoulders.

"You can't go in there, Miss!" he screamed. "The flames'll burn you!"

I watched the house, the inside engulfed in flame, the roof torn off and disposed of in the koi pond. And there, sitting in the exposed attic, hunched forward and camouflaged in the smoke…the dragon watched.

I looked down at my hands. The swirling had stopped, as had the itching… How had I not made the connection before?

It wasn't Miss Witherstine's fault at all…it was mine. The market, the windmill, and—

"James," I whispered. I looked around the gathering crowd, searching for his mop of blond hair. I picked up my skirt and ran around the bend of the wall toward the back roads.

Don't you want this town destroyed?

I stopped, listening. The voice…when had it started asking me questions instead of telling me lies?

I slowly looked up past the crumbled stone wall, the oak tree, and the flaming gardens. The dragon now stood, its form dark except for the glowing orange eyes.

Isn't that what you want?

"No!" I shouted. "No—this is wrong! It's all wrong!"

A sudden cheering came from the front of the property, mixing with the screams and horrified cries from before. The dragon glanced over, and I could have sworn its jaw pulled back into a snarl.

Professor Booker.

My heart stopped. He was back?! I ran around the house again and came to a stop. The Professor stood, his back toward me. His bag and mechanical cane were on the ground next to him, as though he'd dropped it. I could see his wild white hair was exposed, his top hat in his hand. He stared up at the flames, his slender shoulders lowered.

We are not safe.

I…couldn't do this on my own. I needed help. I needed him.

He cannot help you.

I balled my fists.

He will be ashamed of you once he sees who you really are! He will be horrified at the monstrosity you created.

I watched as Professor Booker turned. His eyebrows were scrunched together. His lips pulled together, eyes wide as he searched the crowd. He coughed and stumbled away from the manor.

"Lillian!" he called, waving a hand in front of his face as the smoke filled the air. Then our eyes met. A grin pulled at his lips, and my stomach lurched.

We are not safe here.

"I—" I felt my throat close as a metallic paw wrapped tightly around my middle. I screamed as the beast grabbed me.

"Lillian!" Professor Booker rushed past Miss Witherstine—past the mayor and past the people of Kesterfield. I watched as he ran toward me. My feet left the ground as the dragon took off into the sky. Professor Booker grew smaller and smaller as I got higher and higher into the air. The wind bit at my exposed hands and face. I clung to the sharp metal, my hands itching.

We are not safe.

I curled my toes.

We must protect.

I kept my eyes shut. My hair whipped wildly around my face as I clung to the metal claw that held me. I felt the world shift around me, and suddenly, we had landed. I opened my eyes. The metal claw still gripped me around my middle. I looked at it, struggling to take a deep breath. I recognized my handiwork on the claws—the messy, inconsistent welding. The brass scrap metal I'd snuck from the workshop. The claws that still needed to be buffed and now, more than triple their original size—how had my dragon grown so out of hand so quickly?

I sucked in a breath and looked past the claw at the expanses of Kesterfield.

I could still see the smoke from Miss Witherstine's manor. Thick and inky black and on the other side of a sea of buildings. I blinked and searched around me. The church stood to the right, the steeple proud above the roofs of the rest of the town. I saw the trolley moseying along the cobblestone lanes of the town. The forests and the quarry were past the church and the empty space where the market used to be. I sucked in a breath and looked to my left. I saw Professor Booker's house and the many swirling back roads of Kesterfield. I stood on the top of the workshop.

We must stay safe.

The dragon began to uncurl its mechanical hand, and I screamed. I held on as tight as I could. The muscles in my arms shook.

"We were safe!" I snarled. The beast lowered its head to stare into my eyes. My dragon had indeed grown. Each scale that I'd meticulously placed and welded together had miraculously grown bigger. I narrowed my eyes as I noted the shiny red tint to each scale and gear. This was the stone's doing—it had to be.

I stared into its large, golden-orange eyes.

Were we?

I faltered. Slowly, I lowered my feet and hit the thatched roof. I fell to my knees and dug my fingers into the dry hay. I held on tight as I screamed, "Yes, we—Professor Booker was back and if you hadn't—he could have—"

Professor Booker is not safe.

I stopped.

"What do you mean?"

In a moment, my memory flashed. Sitting in the gutter day after day, night after night. Trying not to listen to the sounds from within the hovel I had called home for so many years of my life.

How long did you live there? How long did he keep you there?

I shook my head and tugged at my braids. "He didn't know! He didn't know I was there, he—"

Pretends to care.

"No!" I screamed, my eyes shut. "No, no, no—"

Was it not him who asked you to lie in the first place?

My throat burned. I sucked in a ragged breath.

Why would he ask you to hide unless shame motivated his actions?

The wind grew hot and stuffy. I slapped my legs to get them to stop shaking.

He is ashamed of you. They all are.

I slipped over the roof to the latched door and threw it open.

Now you are alone again.

I wriggled into the hole and slid into the safety of the work-shop attic.

Now you are truly safe.

I SAT IN THE WORKSHOP'S dusty attic, my knees dragged tight to my chest. On the roof above me, I could hear the metallic gears and crunching footsteps of the beast I had created. I let my head rest against a rung in the ladder behind me and ignored the tears that slipped down my cheeks.

"I've ruined everything," I whispered to the quiet.

"Could be worse."

I jumped at the voice. James stood halfway up the ladder that led down to the second floor. He rested his chin against the top rail.

"*James?*" my voice cracked, and I winced. Dust fluttered down from the roof, and I gasped. "Be careful—the dragon, it's—"

"Connected to you," James frowned. I blinked, and James grinned. "What? You're not the only scientist here. I was the Professor's first assistant…Lillian, do you think I'm a threat?"

I bit my lip.

"Ah," James nodded. My heart ached. With a cautious glance up toward the ceiling, James slowly heaved himself up onto the floor and slipped silently across the room.

He sat beside me, pulled his knees to his chest, and looked at me.

"You okay?" he whispered. I sniffed and nodded. He moved a piece of hair out of my face and then, with his thumb, lightly brushed a scrape along my cheek. He sighed, then asked, "You lyin'?"

My face scrunched, and I nodded again. His arms wrapped around my shoulders as I suppressed quiet sobs.

"After you left me in the forest, I tried to search the other side of town… When I didn't find anything, I came here to give you this."

He reached into his pocket and pulled out a tightly folded, yellow paper. He unfolded the pages, and I immediately recognized the Professor's handwriting. He pressed the paper into my hands. "Here, read it."

I wiped my nose with my sleeve and started to read.

James,

I trust you to accomplish these tasks before my return to the best of your ability.

First, please do whatever you can to help out around the workshop. I have a feeling Miss Witherstine and Lillian won't get along (thus, I've left them each a letter to try and remedy such an outcome, but, you know, women), and therefore, the inventions I've left must be guarded, and taken care of.

The second, you were an apprentice first, so you know how tidy I like things, yet seem incapable of keeping them as such. I know you've taken a step back to help with the Cordington Family Business, but while you're 'hanging around,' please try to clean the house and workshop. Oh, you might say, how do I know you will be 'hanging around'? This leads to the third and final point of discussion I wish to address. I know these three things to be of irrefutable fact.

I love Lillian more than words can describe.

I see the way you look at her.

If you harm her, I will use every invention at my hands to destroy you.

Well wishes,
Professor J. Booker

My cheeks were warm and hot. I wiped the tears and snot from my face and was thankful for how dark the upper attic of the workshop was. Slowly, I passed back the letter.

"So," he coughed. "That's why I…well, in the forest, you said we weren't friends, but…"

He shifted and scratched the back of his neck. Even in the darkened attic space, I could see a faint blush on his cheeks. My stomach clenched.

"So…do you, uh…" he looked away from me. "What do you think of that last paragraph?"

My heart clambered to my throat, and a dull panic beat against my temple. What did I think?

"Professor Booker…loves me?" I whispered. James's nose scrunched as he looked down at the letter and then at me.

"Uh, yeah…but…I mean…he's not the only one."

My breath stuck in my throat. *James…*

He doesn't know what you really are. He can't love you.

The roof groaned. I felt my palms itch.

We are no longer safe.

"James—*run!*" I hissed.

"*What?*"

"Run!"

James looked up at the ceiling—then back into my eyes, his eyebrows pinched together, teeth clenched. The building creaked, and he scrambled across the floor, slipping down the ladder. I shut my eyes and put my hands over my ears.

"It's fine! It's fine!" I whimpered. "He's gone—*he's leaving—it's fine!*"

He knows where we are.

I looked up at the ceiling.

He's going to tell everyone!

I stumbled to my feet as the building trembled. Metallic claws pierced through the roof—straw and dust rained down. I covered my head and ran toward the ladder. Metal groaned. Wood snapped. I stared up as the ceiling was ripped from the windmill like it was a doll house. The dragon craned its neck inside, its teeth flashing in the sunlight. I took a step back. It reached its paw toward me.

Come with me. We must run.

I took another step back.

We must hide.

I turned and ran toward the ladder. Metal gears clicked behind me as I slid down it. I ran toward the staircase.

Why do you run?

I rushed across the second floor and quickly stepped down the stone steps.

"James—" I cut myself off. The door swung on its hinges—James was nowhere in sight.

See? He doesn't really want you. He doesn't love you. Nobody does.

The floor above me cracked. I slapped both hands over my

mouth and rushed toward Professor Booker's workbench. I crouched behind it and went still.

Do you think you can hide from me? We are one. You are a beast, same as me.

I watched the staircase as a glinting metallic claw set foot on the first step. The stone cracked under the weight. I closed my eyes and held my breath.

I am the only one who can keep you safe, Lillian.

Another clank of metal on stone. I squeezed my knees toward my chest and pressed my palms tighter against my lips.

Come out, Lillian...I promise to keep you safe.

I could feel the heat wafting off the dragon's metallic body. I opened my eyes. It stood half in the workshop, its body lodged in the opening. The beast's maw had snapped shut. An orange glow radiated from its middle.

The building suddenly shook, and dust and debris rained down from the ceiling. The dragon stilled, the gears clicked in its head, and then it pulled back and vanished from sight.

I let out a breath. The ground shook again. Slowly, on wobbly legs, I stood and ran toward the still-swinging door. I rested my hand against the wooden door frame and peeked out. The dragon clung to the outside of the workshop—its wings extended, jaw unlatched and open. It hung like a spider in the corner of a web above me. I looked out at the field where the dragon was facing.

Professor Booker stood in the middle of the field. In his hands, he had his arm-cannon. The large brass barrel faced the dragon. The butt of the cannon rested against his right hip. His left hand held the handle on the top of the cannon, and the other squeezed around the trigger on the bottom of it. The metal glinted in the sun. James stood next to him, the bag of head-sized cannonballs at his feet.

"Eat metal!" the Professor cried and pulled the trigger. I watched as the ball erupted from the barrel. It smacked into the dragon's torso and lodged itself in the gears between its legs and body. Smoke rolled out of the barrel of the arm-cannon.

The metal above groaned. James quickly lodged the next cannonball into the barrel and then stooped to the ground to pick up another. I watched as the Professor cracked his neck and shifted the aim.

Behind him was Albert Bamford Jr., who brandished two brass pistols, one in each hand.

A large crowd formed behind them on the road.

Stay back!

I looked up. Above me, the dragon clung to the outside of the workshop. Its tail flicked behind it, the blades in its shoulder grinding as it slunk down the outside of the building and curled in front of the workshop. Between me and Professor Booker.

I will protect you.

I heard a click—the dragon unhinged its jaw. My eyes widened.

"*Get away!*" I shrieked. Seconds later, flames barreled from the dragon and scorched the barren field. I rushed away from the door and slammed it shut.

What should I do? I sucked in a breath and pulled at my braids. I looked at all of Professor Booker's inventions. From the destroyed Dust-In propped up in the corner to the half-finished flying machine to the left. No, no, none of them would work! I smacked the side of my head and turned in a circle.

"Oh, crackers! Think, Lillian, think!" I grit my teeth. "Oh, my—"

I stopped as my foot splashed in a puddle. I looked down at the ground, and followed the small stream of water across the floor, up the bookcase, to the drawer.

I gasped and quickly moved across the room. The wood was soaked on the outside. I gripped the metal handle—cool to the touch. I tugged. Inside, atop a small pile of slushy snow, sat the fourth and final stone. The icy white glow illuminated the edges of the drawer. I grit my teeth and snatched it up. Immediately, the chill set deep into the bones of my fingers. I hissed as I rushed back to the door. I flew out, stumbled on the cracked dirt, and stopped. The dragon loomed in front of me, its back toward me. I took six quick steps around its side, reared my arm back, and threw the stone.

It flew through the air and the stone shattered against the beast's lower left jaw. Immediately, a bright white light began to shine from the shattered pieces. The light overtook the orange of the flames, and the air around us grew cold. I stumbled back as crackling ice like lightning shot across the creature's metal surface. The gears stopped and clicked—the creature froze in place. A large ice block encased its head.

I sucked in a breath and let it out. I watched the cloud escape my lips. The grass beneath my feet was still warm and charred black. I held my right hand with my left—the skin icy and red. It throbbed. Across the field, Professor Booker and The Defense Team stared up at the dragon, mouths agape.

"Professor!" I called. My heart hammered, and a grin poked at my cheeks. I pointed. I'd done it! "I froze it— look, did you see? I—"

A crack echoed around the field. I let my hand fall to my side and looked up at the dragon. Its orange eyes glowed from inside the ice as it stared directly at me. The chest plate on its torso glowed orange. Drops of water began leaking from the rocks of ice.

What are you doing?

I stepped back. Another crack appeared in the ice. Gears began to click. I sucked in a breath and took another step away.

I am protecting you—I am trying to protect you!

"You aren't protecting me," I yelled. "You're keeping me away from everybody!"

They were going to find out the truth. You can't tell them the truth. They'll never forgive you for lying.

I scoffed. "I'm not lying, I'm…"

I pressed my lips together.

I *was* lying—about everything! About Professor Booker and my birth. Since when had lies become more comfortable than the truth?

If the dragon was protecting my lies, then only one thing could get it to stop.

The ice cracked again. I took a step back. I looked down at my hands. The angry red scratches pulsed with a dull maroon light. I clenched my hands into fists and looked up at my dragon. Its head twisted as the ice block shattered. Its jaw unclenched and it spit a fiery burst of flame into the sky.

I shuffled backward and cupped my hands around my mouth. "James! I *did* lie to you—I'm *not* okay!"

What are you doing?

The metal head veered toward me. I turned and fled toward the town. I heard Professor Booker shout my name—the ground shook. I glanced behind me. The dragon bounded toward me, its jaw latched, wings folded against its body. I jumped over the gardens and through the iron gate.

This is unacceptable!

I heard the metallic whirring of wings and saw a shadow overtake the pathway ahead of me. I veered to the right and into the forest. Twigs snapped at my cheeks and leaves tugged at my hair as I continued to run as fast as I could toward town.

I huffed out a breath as I met cobblestone roads once more. The church loomed in front of me. I grinned and took off down the road.

You think that any of them will accept you if they knew?

I tore up the steps and through the large wooden doors. I barely spared Mother Mary a glance as I raced down the pews and to the stairway in the back right corner. The building shook. I stumbled and leaned against the wall.

Do you think they will love you?

I grunted as I stood and kept climbing. I burst into the top of the steeple—the bell that was turned on its side. At the top of the bell, closest to me, was the speaker Professor Booker had invented. A small port where you spoke faced me, the pipes leading to the bell where your voice would be magnified and spread through all of Kesterfield. I took a moment to take in the town. Brass pipes sprawled out like a spiderweb upon every surface of the town, into every home. The market lay in front of me, still singed and charred black. Empty, broken stalls and without a single person to be seen inside it. Behind me, to the left, large plumes of smoke rose into the sky from Creekstone Manor.

The building shook. I looked behind me. The dragon stood

on the roof, its wings stretched out, its jaw unhooked and open. I heard a click. I ran toward the machine.

I pressed my mouth against the bell. Another click. I screwed my eyes shut.

"My name is Lillian Booker!" My voice echoed through the town past the crackling speaker. "I'm not Professor Booker's niece—I'm his *daughter*."

Silence.

Slowly, I opened my eyes. The dragon stood still, and I watched as the orange glow faded from its eyes. I sucked in a breath.

They will never accept you. You've ruined...everything.

Then, slowly, the dragon whined. It tilted its head to the left and then tumbled off the roof.

I released my finger from the speaker and clutched it to my chest. I listened as metal clattered to the ground. I shut my eyes, my hands pulsed, and then, finally, the incessant itching that had ruled my life for three days stopped. I looked down at my palms and watched the glowing maroon specks fade to a dull gray.

I walked almost as though caught in a trance. Down the steps, past Mother Mary and her babe, through the pews, and out the doors.

It was only as I stepped down the steps of the church and the wind tickled my cheeks that I realized I was crying. Big tears slipped down my cheeks, clung to my chin, and then leaped off my face to the ground. I walked around the church and came to a stop.

The dragon sat frozen on the ground, back to its original size.

Small and frozen, with dull marble eyes. I walked forward, up

the small grassy hill, until I came face to face with the beast…
with my dragon. The brass almost seemed to glitter in the dying
rays of the sunset. I reached out a hand and tentatively tugged
on the jaw. Its mouth was stuck shut. The wings had curled
in on themselves. The tail was still sharp, the claws should've
been buffed and chiseled down—rounded out. The eyes had oil
smeared on them.

I wrapped my arms around the frozen creature, now a statue
once more, and sobbed.

There is no safety in vulnerability. There is no safety in being known.

And there is no love in isolation.

Behind me, I heard the gravel crunch. Professor Booker and
James stood at a distance. They eyed the dragon and me wari-
ly. I gave them my best attempt at a smile and found no energy
to hide my tears.

"Oh, darling," Professor Booker whispered. He walked forward, his cane discarded, his clothes singed. He knelt next
to me and wrapped me in a hug. I wrapped my arms tightly
around his neck and let myself release all I had carried.

"I'm sorry," I whispered. I shut my eyes and rested my forehead on his shoulder. *"I'm sorry."*

THREE WEEKS LATER, I found myself inside the church once more. I sat in the pew. My back rested against Professor Booker's side, his arm draped over my shoulder. I stared ahead and listened intently to the preacher.

"And thus the Scripture says, 'I will forgive their unrighteousness, and remember their unlawful sins no more,'" the preacher thumped his Bible. "And so I say to you, people, forgiveness is the backbone of our good and perfect town of Kesterfield!"

The congregation's reaction was a mixture of quiet huffs and gentle applause. I glanced briefly at the Mother Mary's curving features. She cradled a babe in her arms, her eyes watching carefully over the congregation in the church.

In the front row, Albert sat with Iris. Their courtship had been announced just two weeks prior, directly after Miss Witherstine removed herself from her self-appointed role of sole benefactor of Booker Enterprises.

It was a financial loss that hit us hard, but one I was sure we could recover from. After all, Professor Booker was practically a celebrity in Kesterfield. People were eager for his inventions, no matter his past.

"Amen."

I snapped to attention as the preacher concluded the service. We stood and joined the throng of people gathering at the back, next to the doors.

"Ah, Professor Booker—Professor Booker." I glanced up as the mayor approached us. I smiled, my hands clasped behind my back. The mayor settled next to the Professor and placed a hand on his shoulder. "Tell me, what are you and Lillian doing this evening? Albert and I have questions—more questions, yes. For the both of you on the-the machines—they could be used to protect the city, no? Instead of putting the young men in needless danger a-against the beasts from the quarry."

"We'd love to come—oh, Lillian, please—fetch James. Let him know where we'll be dining tonight." Professor Booker patted me on the shoulder. "I'll see you back at the workshop."

I leaned in and gave the professor a quick hug. He squeezed my shoulder, and I stepped back as he engaged in conversation with the mayor. Quietly, I slipped out the doors of the church. My skirts and hair fluttered in the wind as I looked over the town of Kesterfield.

Repairs had already been started on the market and Miss Witherstine's manor. Professor Booker had ensured her the manor would be restored brighter and better than it had originally been.

"I've seen more daring escapes in my day. But as far as going unnoticed, a banger job, really."

I looked to my right. James stood there with a crooked grin. I smiled and stepped down the stone steps of the church.

"Oh, how do you do, Mr. Cordington," I dipped my head and gave an exaggerated curtsy. James's sly smirk cracked into a grin as he bowed.

"Very well, Miss Booker, very well." He strolled up next to me and offered his elbow. I accepted it, and together, the two of us strolled through the town. "How are your hands?"

"Healing quite nicely, according to Professor Booker." I nodded and looked down at my palms. It'd taken the professor, James, and myself hours to remove every last bit of dust. Even still, bandages were wrapped around each finger.

Together, we walked through the market.

My heart, finally, was at peace… There were still dangers to face, but I knew now I wouldn't be doing it alone.

Sometimes, I still heard the voice. The insidious whisper that insisted on speaking lies to my heart. But I knew what the truth was now. I looked up at James, and he smiled back. Together, we boarded the trolley, which rumbled down the lane toward the workshop.

Now, I knew that I was loved—not for who I pretended to be—but for who I was.

DID YOU LOVE *COPPER LIES*?

Tell somebody about it! Share the book with a friend and leave a review on Amazon or Goodreads.

Your honest review helps other people find great books that they'll love.

Thanks for enjoying the work of Alli Prince!

ACKNOWLEDGMENTS

THIS BOOK WOULDN'T EXIST if my love for story had not been meticulously cared for. So first and foremost, I want to thank my mom and dad. You saw a small, eight-year-old girl scribbling down her imaginations and, instead of telling her to go get a real job or to stop wasting the printer paper, you sat with her and fanned the flame of creativity.

To my best friend, Shelby Little, who listened every time I called her on the phone, crying about how much this story sucked and would never be published. You never gave up on me, even when I gave up on me. Thank you.

To my sister, Katelyn, who, in my time of need, came up with the title for this book.

A huge thank you to everyone in my church, Redeeming Passion Ministries, for loving on me and encouraging me in my writing, but a special shout out to Raina Daniels, Breanna Siburt, Teagan Barrone, and Daphne Woodmansee. Your friendship inspires me every single day. Thank you for showing me the love of Christ.

Thank you to Vella Karman for working on the copy edit, to

R.J. Catlin for working on the interior design and to Levi Matthews for the cover! You all helped bring this book together.

A huge thank you to Brad and Melissa Pauquette. Your mentorship and guidance encouraged and uplifted me. You both have made such an impact on my life and on this story. Thank you.

This book wouldn't have been produced, had it not been for my monthly supporters, so a huge thank you to Christina Silic, David Bartlett, David and Lydia Silic, Catherine Stringer, Heidi Thornhill, Kevin Prince, Katelyn Flatt, and Sam and Reece. Without your support this book wouldn't have made it off my computer. Thank you!

And most importantly, I want to thank God. His love is so present, everlasting, and never changing. It is only because of his steadfast love that I stand, that I breath, that I live.

Dear reader, never forget that he is madly in love with you. *You* are his beloved.

About the Author

ALLI PRINCE has been creating stories since she could form words and has been writing long before she learned about sentence structure and grammar (her editors think she could still learn a thing or two about grammar). She's been published to *The Pearl* and was the project manager for *Lawless*.

Alli is a graduate of The Company and is currently completing a one-year internship there. She is learning everything she can about writing, editing, and marketing. She hopes to use these skills to influence the world of Christian literature and bring glory to God's name.

Alli lives in Cambridge, Ohio, but is originally from Las Vegas, Nevada, where her family of twelve (yes, you read that right, twelve) cheer her on and encourage her to pursue the dreams God has placed on her heart. To learn more about her, check out her Instagram @alliprinceauthor or visit her website alliprince.com.

JOIN HER NEWSLETTER AT ALLIPRINCE.COM AND NEVER MISS A FUTURE RELEASE!

More from the imagination of
Alli Prince

Enjoy the work of Alli Prince, with thirteen other authors, in this gritty, imaginative sci-fi anthology based on the biblical book of Judges.

Available wherever great books are sold!
LawlessBook.com

Scan for Amazon

Ready for another great adventure?

ONE MISTAKE. TWO EMPIRES. COUNTLESS SECRETS.
A high-stakes game of deception full of mercenaries, emperors, and sweet romance. Start the *Adventures in Eldnaire* trilogy today.

Available wherever great books are sold!
PearlBooks.co

Scan for Amazon

Ready to write like Alli?

Alli Prince graduated from The Company's apprenticeship in 2024. If you're ready to kick your writing into gear, check it out at:
Writers.Company

Don't stop now.
More great stories are just around the corner.

New short stories, essays, and poetry posted weekly. Read and subscribe today at
PearlMag.co